Revelations in Serendipity

SERENDIPITY SUNSETS BOOK FOUR

LIZA LANTER

Also By

Contents

CHAPTER ONE

Jenn

"SCORE ONE FOR THE sisters being right. We said that Dawson never stopped loving Amber." Renee chuckled under her breath while drinking her first cup of coffee the morning after Amber's arrival in Serendipity.

"I'm thrilled at the news." Jenn responded, drinking the strongest dark roast variety she could find that morning. "I'm stunned at the timing."

"Yes, announcing a wedding hours after checking out of rehab is an interesting turn of events. Amber's always been one to go her own way. If she wanted to get married to someone she met in rehab, we might have to intervene. Remarrying the man who appears to unconditionally love her, is the father of her child, and who most people think is freaking wonderful on all levels, is hard to build a case against."

Letting Amber sleep in, Neil had taken Dawson and Willis with him to the condo building worksite in Tyrell County. In the construction business himself in California, Dawson was eager to see Neil's latest project. Willis didn't seem to object to going along, especially when the teenager was promised a big breakfast.

"We've got to work on improving her health. She is scarily skinny. I see fruit and veggie smoothies every morning with protein powder." Jenn started making a mental grocery list.

"With bacon and hashbrowns." Renee added. "And pancakes. Mom's blueberry pancakes with maple syrup."

"Can I have that now?"

For a moment, Amber's soft voice sounded like it did when she was a little girl. Before Jenn turned around, she pictured her little sister in her Minnie Mouse nightgown with bunny slippers and her mussed bedhead hair. The woman she now saw standing in the doorway looked small and vulnerable like the younger version. Amber needed all the sisterly love that Jenn and Renee could give her. They were up for the challenge.

"Good morning, sleepyhead." Renee rose from her chair. "I can't do exactly what I mentioned, but I can make you a plate of food that will remind you of our childhood."

"Sounds good. I think I could eat some breakfast with my sissies."

Making eye contact with Renee, Jenn smiled remembering their years of growing up together. Having Amber as a younger sister helped prepare Jenn for her own youngest child. There was something about the third child that made him or her different.

Jenn had decided earlier in the week that she was going to work from home on Amber's first full day with them. Both she and Renee knew that long walks on the beach and even longer conversations were needed. Jenn could not remember the last time that the three of them had a heart-to-heart talk. Secrets needed to be revealed.

While Jenn opened her laptop, checking her email for pressing topics or messages from Doris, Renee began working on the ingredients for omelets. Green bell peppers, white mushrooms, spring onions, Roma tomatoes, and baby spinach waited for someone to chop into bite size morsels to sauté.

"Remember what Mom used to say?" Renee laid a chopping board and knife in front of Amber.

"If you work for the meal, it tastes better."

Amber slid off the chair she'd been sitting on at the counter and began slicing the pepper, then chopping the slices into bite-size pieces. With her back to Renee who was cooking sausage on the stove, Jenn could see a tear running down Amber's face.

While they did not grow up in the beach house, it became their parents' home shortly after the three sisters reached adulthood. The kitchen was the heart of Paisley Halston's domain. It was one of the hardest aspects of living in the house for Jenn. While they hadn't discussed the topic, Jenn imagined it was the same for Renee. Their mother's sudden death had been the catalyst to Amber's relapse. Jenn wanted to make sure her time with them was about coming to grips with their shared loss and healing.

"I'm going to take Jasper out for a short walk while you two make breakfast."

"Jenn's breakfast won't taste as good as ours, Amber." Renee winked at Jenn.

"You seemed to have forgotten that I did the grocery shopping this week. I bought everything you two are preparing. That's my 'work' in this scenario." Jenn nodded her head in agreement with what she said before leaving.

Once Jenn and Jasper were down the steps and walking down the driveway, Jenn noticed that an unfamiliar vehicle was parked behind Gladys' car. Looking up at her neighbor's house, she saw a man sitting on the upper deck, talking on his cell phone. Seeing Jenn, the man rose, waved, and started walking down the steps toward her.

"Hello, Jenn? You probably don't remember me. I'm Gladys' nephew, Wade. Wade Stanley." The young man extended his hand to Jenn.

"Oh, my goodness! It's been a long time, Wade." Jenn shook his hand. "Gladys didn't mention that she was expecting a visitor."

"She wasn't expecting me. I called her yesterday on my way here. It's a long story, but the short version is that it's a new world we are living in. My company is moving its headquarters, and I have the option to be more mobile in where I live. I always enjoyed my summers with Aunt Gladys, so I decided to consider Serendipity, or one of the towns nearby."

Jenn took in the young man's appearance while he spoke. Like she remembered, Wade was tall. His once lanky build had filled out with broad shoulders and strong arms. Claire would be impressed with how her first love turned out. Jenn remembered his brown hair being longer in his teens. His hair now was slightly long on top with almost a buzzcut style on the sides and back. Wade's eyes matched his hair. Jenn thought they might be the same color as Gladys'.

"That certainly seems like a popular choice these days. Do you remember my son, Foster?"

"Absolutely! He's the one who taught me how to surf. Is he living here now? I think I remember that you all were living in Atlanta when we were growing up."

"That's right. Foster and his wife lived in Atlanta until about a month ago. His job also allows him to basically live anywhere that's near an international airport. After I moved back to Serendipity earlier this year, Foster and Michelle decided to come, too."

"That's great. How's Claire doing?"

There was a smile in Wade's eyes when he said Claire's name. Jenn remembered her oldest daughter's teenage romance with this young man. He was a year older than Claire and spending the summer in Serendipity. Claire was head-over-heels for him. They'd kept in touch for a while via email and occasional phone calls, but it was a long way from Atlanta to Boston and not much opportunity for the teenagers to see each other again.

"Claire is doing well. She's an art buyer for a large gallery in Atlanta."

"Great! She was already quite into art the summer we met. We lost touch after I got into college. I'm happy to hear that she is living her dream. I guess she still lives with her family in Atlanta then?"

Jenn wondered how far Wade would go with his questions to find out what he wanted to know, or if he'd already asked Gladys similar ones.

"She's getting ready to move here as well. Being an art buyer, she travels all over the world to make purchases for the gallery. Her other time is spent researching and negotiating those purchases. Claire's another one who needs an international airport and good internet service, but not a specific geographic location."

"How ironic is that?" Wade looked toward the direction of the ocean. "I would imagine that her family doesn't object to living at the beach after the city life of Atlanta."

For the second time in two sentences, Wade had used the word 'family' in reference to Claire. He was trying to be nonchalant with his 'fishing expedition,' but Jenn hadn't taken the bait.

"Most people love the beach."

Jasper laid down at Jenn's feet. He was ready to go back inside.

"Please tell Claire that I said hello. Maybe once she gets settled, I can see her and meet her family."

"Wade, I'm not going to torture you any longer. One of the reasons that Claire is moving here is because she's getting a divorce. She does not have any children."

Wade raised his eyebrows in a surprised expression.

"Claire was married to a delightful young man she met in college. It didn't work out. She's starting a new chapter with Serendipity as the home base."

"That sounds wonderful. I'd love to see her and catch up. It's been almost a dozen years, I guess, since that summer."

Jenn noticed a faraway look in Wade's eyes. His mouth turned up in a slight smile.

"It was lovely to see you again. I apologize for calling you Jenn. Aunt Gladys told me that you were recently divorced and had taken back the Halston name, so I didn't think that calling you Mrs. Young was quite appropriate."

"I would have made a face, if you had." Jenn laughed. "Then, I would have told you to call me Jenn. I will certainly tell Claire that her old friend is hanging around on the beach again. Maybe we can stage a reunion."

"I would enjoy that. Old friends understand you in a way that newer ones cannot."

Wade's words rang true. The sentiment made Jenn think of her own old friends who had become important newer versions.

"Tell Gladys that we expect her to come and visit with my sister, Amber, whenever she can."

"I will tell her. She mentioned that all three of the Halston sisters were reunited under one roof. From what she has told me, your family certainly has a great deal to celebrate. I remember Claire telling me about her cousin who had been abducted. It's an amazing story that he has been found after all these years."

"You will have to meet him, too. Joe is living in Serendipity as well. He's joined our local police department."

"How fitting for someone with such a tragic experience to want to be a defender of others. Bravo!"

"Good to talk to you, Wade. I look forward to seeing you again soon."

With Jasper on her heels, Jenn climbed up the steps and returned to the kitchen.

"I was about to come looking for you. I just flipped the hashbrowns, so breakfast is almost ready."

"I ran into Gladys' nephew. I didn't realize she was having a guest."

"Are you *sure* it was her nephew?" Renee gave Jenn a stern look. "We've had a run of impersonators in our neighborhood lately."

"I'm sure about this one. I've met him before. Wade looks the same, only older. About a dozen years ago, he spent the summer with Gladys. Claire and Foster were also spending the same summer with Mom and Dad. He and Claire had a little 'summer love.'"

"Oh, I remember that. Mom talked about how sweet it was to watch. They kept in touch for a while, didn't they?"

"Yes. They exchanged emails and phone calls. I remember that Claire was mortified when I suggested that she write Wade a letter. Apparently, that was the epitome of uncool at the time."

"It would be even worse with kids today." Amber sat down at the kitchen table with her plate of food. "Waiting for a letter to come through the postal service would seem like an eternity compared to the instantaneousness of a text or similar message."

"I remember having a pen pal in London when I was in elementary school." Renee handed Jenn a plate of food. "It would take over two weeks for a letter to make its way 'across the pond.' A lot can change in a young heart in two weeks."

"Anyway, Wade mentioned that he and Claire lost touch when he went off to college. Wade is from Boston. That's a long way from Atlanta."

"How long is he visiting for? It would certainly be a nice surprise if Claire could see her old friend." Bringing her own meal and a plate of toasted English muffins, Renee sat down with her sisters.

"Wade is moving here. He also has one of those jobs that can be done from anywhere now."

"Remote working has quickly become the future." Renee poured each of them a small glass of orange juice from a carafe. "I would imagine it is easier to up and move to another part of the country if you are single. Is Wade single?" Renee raised one eyebrow.

"You know, I was about to say yes, but I really don't know. He quite slyly kept asking me questions about Claire, but I never asked Wade any about himself. I don't even know what type of work he does." Jenn scowled. "I totally failed that assignment. I'm going to blame it on being caught off guard."

"A true reporter is always ready to get the facts of a story." Renee shook her finger at Jenn. "Madam Publisher, you are going to have to work on those skills if you want to keep up with your staff and your family!"

"I'm sure I will have better skills on a full stomach." Jenn took her first bite of the omelet. "Oh, Big Sister, this is delicious. What makes the eggs so creamy and fluffy?"

"Beating them in a blender." Renee answered, after her first bite of English muffin. "Plus, I also add ricotta cheese. Where in the world did this strawberry jam come from? It tastes like a fresh strawberry."

"I buy it at The Frosted Goddess. I believe the owner makes it. Her name is Jasmine. She also has peach and fig versions that I haven't tried yet."

"I agree with Renee, it's like eating fresh strawberries. It's not gooey like most jams are." Amber spread a healthy amount of the jam onto her half-eaten English muffin. "You might want to hide this from Dawson. He might eat it right out of the jar." Amber giggled.

"Look at that glowing smile on her face, Jenn." Renee raised one eyebrow. "If I didn't know better, I'd say our little sister was in love."

"Ah, Renee, I think that was the whole point of that surprising announcement last night."

"I should have known better than to stay in touch with those women."

After Jenn and her sisters took a long walk on the beach to burn some of the calories of their breakfast, the three sat in chairs on the beach enjoying a rare warmer day before winter set in.

"Most of the basketball wives were great. Some had a little bit of a diva side, but they were basically good people. A couple had addictive personalities. It was always about what they had or what they were buying next. Some came from extremely poor childhoods, as did their husbands. Once they had money, they wanted to spend it—spend it to excess."

Wrapped up in a throw on a beach chair, Amber began telling the story about how her addiction began.

"It started out so innocently. We would get together while our husbands were playing on the road. Someone would bring a sampling of a certain drug just for the others to try. I'd never been exposed to such before. It was foreign to me. I didn't want to be the odd one out by not trying it. I wanted to be one of the 'cool' wives. Dawson knew nothing about it. I don't think he even suspected that I had a problem until he came home one day and found a dealer sitting outside our front door. I'd recently told him that I thought I was pregnant, so I wouldn't buy anything from the dealer. The guy didn't want to leave without a sale. Once Dawson was through with him, he left."

"We didn't know any of this, Amber. We would have helped you." Renee's expression was one of sadness.

"That was a benefit of being in California. All the people who *really* knew me were three thousand miles away. It was easy to hide it, until it was not." Amber sighed. "It tore our marriage apart. Dawson didn't want any part of it. He never left my side though. Even when we were no longer living together, he was always there, watching out for Willis and I."

"We've always known that Dawson was a good man."

"A good man stuck with your train wreck sister."

"Stop talking like that!" Renee's tone was tinged with anger. "We've never said those type of words, and you can't either. You've been troubled and had times of weakness. It doesn't mean that you don't have the strength to overcome these issues."

"Exactly! We are going to help you." Jenn raised her fist in the air.

"I really thought I had beaten it until Mom died."

"Oh, Amber, Mom passing so suddenly did a number on all of us." Jenn reached over, taking Amber's hand in hers. "You're never prepared to lose your mother. In our case, it was way too sudden, way too soon."

"She would love us being here together." From the other side, Renee squeezed Amber's hand before releasing it. "You've got plenty of that

Halston and Frederick spunk in you. Wait until you see Aunt Rachel. She will inspire you. The woman is a fireball—full of spit and vinegar."

"Just like our mother." Amber choked back tears.

"Yes, Aunt Rachel is more like Mom than we realized." Jenn released Amber's hand, turning her chair to better face both sisters. "You know, Doris reminded me the other day that Aunt Rachel will be eighty-five on her next birthday."

"Oh, that's right. Such a momentous occasion calls for a celebration. We need to plan a party and I know just the location for it." Renee gave Jenn a wide-eyed look.

"Oh, we couldn't!" Jenn shook her head, negatively, then tilted it in a questioning manner. "Could we?"

"You're the one who mentioned that the lawyers said we could have access to it."

"Access. No one said we could throw a party there." Jenn's mind raced with possibilities.

"Did anyone say we couldn't?" Renee had a glimmer in her eyes.

"What in the world are you two talking about?" Amber looked from Jenn to Renee and back again.

"I guess we could ask Mr. Wolff."

"Am I not mistaken that Thurgood Wolff was sweet on Aunt Rachel after his wife passed years ago? Didn't Mother tell us about them keeping company for a while?" Renee stood up.

"Now that you mention it, I think you're right." Jenn stood up, too.

"Where are you thinking about having a party for Aunt Rachel? Who is Thurgood Wolff?"

"Oh, little sister, we've got a lot to talk about."

Jenn and Renee sat back down in their chairs and began to tell Amber the story of the strange neighbor next door and how that led them to the Oasis.

"Dawson, you are not going to believe what Jenn and Renee told me today about the house next door."

After grilling hamburgers and hotdogs, the family braved a windy evening to eat outdoors.

"I think I will believe it because Neil told me the incredible story already. What generous people the Bentleys were and how much they must have thought of you three!"

"They were like family to us, no doubt." Amber sat down between Dawson and Willis. "It doesn't surprise me that they left us something. I'm like Jenn; I would have imagined it might be a piece of art from Mrs. Bentley's collection or even some shares in one of the companies that Mr. Bentley believed in. I *never* would have dreamed they would leave us the Oasis. It's like Elvis leaving us Graceland."

"I don't believe we will be able to get as many visitors to Serendipity as go to Memphis." Renee laughed at Amber's comparison. "I do think that, like Graceland, the Oasis is a special place, and we need to make a sound decision about what to do with it going forward."

"We were going to wait until you'd been here over twenty-four hours before we talked to you about this, Amber, but since we are all here, we might as well tell you our initial idea." Jenn glanced at Renee. Her sister shook her head, encouragingly. "We've thought about turning it into a high-end resort to be run by our sister who specializes in hospitality."

Amber's eyes grew big with surprise. A smile crossed Dawson's face. Willis was the one to verbalize.

"Does that mean we would move to the beach?"

"Oh, you two, that's crazy. I've not done that type of work for a long time. I couldn't do that."

"Why not? That's exactly what you were doing when I met you." Dawson put his arm around Amber. "You were running a property that was considerably larger than the one next door."

"We've been planning to go back to California. Your business is there."

"We've also talked about making a new start. My business runs itself now. Haven't you heard? There's a family construction business on this side of the country that's even bigger and might be hiring."

"That business would definitely hire you!" Neil placed a platter of hamburgers and hotdogs in the center of the table.

"I thought this was a private beach area. Can you even run a business in this neighborhood?"

"The zoning has allowed it for decades." Jenn placed a bowl of salad and a platter of buns on the table before she sat down. "There are already rental properties about a half mile in each direction."

"Amber, we don't have to make a quick decision. There are still several legal hoops before it will be deeded to us anyway. We told you that there is a trust that goes with it to take care of expenses. The fact remains that at some point we will need to do something with the property. We can't just let it sit there empty." Renee began passing food around the table.

"I'm hoping that there may be more information once we officially inherit it. Perhaps Mr. Bentley left a letter regarding his ideas, if the property ended up passing to us. He was a thorough sort of person. He might have left some guidance."

"Good thoughts, Jenn. That sounds like something he might have done."

"It's so overwhelming." Amber shook her head.

"But, my darling, you will have your two sisters by your side." Dawson took hold of her hand. "Willis and I will be right beside you every step of the way. Won't we, buddy?"

"Absolutely, Mom! You can do this. I'd love to move here." Willis poured chili on his two hotdogs.

Gazing at everyone around the table, Jenn caught Renee's eye. The two shared an understanding smile. *This family could do anything...together.*

CHAPTER TWO

Randy

"I saw one of the district attorneys from Raleigh the other day at a meeting."

Edwin Greer, Serendipity's District Attorney, sat across the table from Randy. It was a rare lunch meeting for the two men. Randy and Edwin handed the La Siesta menus back to the server after placing their orders.

"Those guys have their hands full all the time, don't they?" Randy looked at the tables around them in the crowded restaurant.

"They certainly do. This case involving Joe Davenport is going to be a doozy though. Has anyone shared with you the background they've already discovered about the man who abducted him?"

"I've heard bits and pieces. Woodrow Fairfield seems to have had a torrid past." Randy lowered his voice.

"I'll say. He was a henchman for one of the larger mafia syndicates on the East Coast. Apparently, he was good at doing the dirty work, like abducting people."

"Since he abducted a child, I wondered if he might have been involved in child trafficking or something like that."

"He was slick with the process he used to take Joe from that elementary school." Randy took a drink of iced tea. "Somehow, Woodrow managed to take Joe without anyone seeing him. I've asked Joe and he has no memory of the moment he was taken. He does have a memory of waking up in the backseat of a strange car. Woodrow must have used something to knock him out quickly. From what some of the investigators have told me they can't find anything that indicates that Woodrow made a habit of taking children though. Samantha Fairfield told the investigators that Woodrow was more of a hitman. Joe was the only child that she knows of who Woodrow ever kidnapped."

"I've heard that, too. That kind of information is not going to bode well for Samantha Fairfield. She's basically told investigators that she asked Woodrow to get her a child. There doesn't seem to be any evidence that Samantha was an accomplice in the crime, but it is certainly apparent that she was an accessory after the fact and for the next twenty years." Edwin poured creamer into his coffee. "Considering her age, I imagine she will spend the rest of her life in prison."

"That's what I think. I'm not sure how Joe is going to take that. This is the woman who raised him, who he knew as his mother."

"There's nothing easy about this for Joe, that's for sure. I imagine that his parents are going to have some conflicting feelings about Samantha Fairfield as well. She took care of Joe and kept him alive all these years. You and I both know that's a rare outcome in these types of situations."

"Indeed. I think that Renee and Neil also fully understand that Samantha Fairfield could have ended this situation a long time ago. Woodrow has been dead for quite a while. Joe is an adult."

"You refer to Joe's parents like you know them personally, Randy." Edwin nodded to the server while his food was placed in front of him.

"Thank you. Could I have some sour cream?" Randy eyeballed his burrito plate. "I've known Renee all my life. We grew up on the same street. I've only met Neil recently, but he's a real solid guy."

"I understand that you've been seeing the new owner of the *Serendipity Sun*. She's Joe's aunt, right? I've not met her yet."

"Yes, Jenn Halston is the new owner of the newspaper. She is Renee Davenport's sister. Jenn is the one who figured out who Joe is because of his resemblance, at that age, to his father."

"Am I correct that she's also the one who tipped off authorities about the person who was impersonating Walter Bentley's grandson?"

"That's correct, too. She's had some interesting experiences since she returned to Serendipity."

"Sounds like you should hire her as an investigator." Edwin chuckled.

"I think Jenn's rather focused on running the newspaper right now."

"Rumor also has it that her return to our town has taken one of Serendipity's most eligible bachelors off the market. Is that an accurate statement, Chief?"

Randy could tell from the expression on his friend's face that Edwin was enjoying the conversation a little more than Randy wanted.

"You must have been talking to some of my officers."

"Someone from your team is on my witness stand almost every week. I've heard about that incident which occurred on Main Street a month or two ago. I'm going to have to check the town code and see if there's still an ordinance on the books about public displays of affection." Edwin almost choked on his food he was laughing so hard.

"Don't expect me to administer the Heimlich maneuver if you get choked on your ribbing, Edwin."

"I've got to give you a little bit of a hard time, man. You have been the topic of more than one dinner conversation at my house through the years, buddy. My wife's had a list of women she'd like to fix you up with on a date. I've told her repeatedly that I don't want to be in your love life. You and I need to stay friends."

"I appreciate that. I've gone on my share of blind dates through the years. Jenn, well, she's the real thing. Since we are old friends, I'll be as frank with my answer as I can." Randy finished swallowing. "If I'd been smart when I was a kid, I would have married her back then. I don't intend to make the same mistake twice."

"That serious, huh?"

"Yes. I am."

"I'll quit giving you a hard time then. You're a good man. You do a lot for this community. You deserve some happiness."

"Thank you. That comment might have earned you a free lunch, Mr. District Attorney."

"How has your visit with Amber been going?"

Earlier in the day, Randy asked Jenn to stop by his house for a quick dinner on her way home. He relished whatever time alone they could manage.

"It's been great. Amber is exhausted though, a deep mental exhaustion. I think it's been an emotional rollercoaster for her to be in that house with Renee and me. The memories of our parents are strong. It makes Mom's sudden passing fresh again. Plus, she's been reconnecting with Dawson and Willis. I'm not sure if Amber was prepared to see her ex-husband and son so quickly after leaving rehab. Did I tell you that they've decided to head back to California tomorrow?"

"No. I wouldn't have asked you to have dinner if I'd known this was your last night with her."

"That's okay. The three of them are flying out early in the morning, but Amber is returning in about a week. Willis needs to get back to school. Dawson has some things to deal with regarding his business. They are thinking about getting a place here, eventually. I think there will be some commuting until the Christmas school break."

"What about Amber and Dawson getting remarried?"

"That's still the plan as far as I know. They are going to take things slow. Which will give Amber some time to continue working on her recovery. Her counselor at the rehab center told us that it's crucial for Amber to deal with the issues that made her relapse. The main trigger was Mom's passing. Staying at the house with us will force her to work through some of those issues."

"You each have dealt with difficult situations over the last year. I get the impression that it's been a long while since the three of you have spent an extended amount of time together." Randy began to serve Jenn from a large pot of spaghetti on the stove. "I hope you're hungry. This is a big pot of my firehouse spaghetti."

"I'm starving. It smells delicious." Jenn accepted the plate from Randy, then sat down at the nearby table. "Renee and I have kept in better touch with each other than with Amber. She was on the West Coast for so long. It made time together difficult. Honestly, the three of us haven't been together for more than four or five days since we all lived in the same house."

"Oh, that will be interesting." Randy sat across from Jenn with his own plate of food. "Three sisters in the same house."

"Since we are all older, we can hope that our teenage argument days are behind us. I often reflected on those years when all three of my children were still at home. The age gap between Claire and Foster and their little sister, Emily, reminded me of the way it was with Renee and I regarding Amber."

"I can't say that I remember too much about Amber while we were growing up. The age difference is more pronounced when you are younger. I do recall that she was quite athletic."

"Yes, Amber was a strong runner. She competed on the state level every year of high school. I've been thinking that could be something that she and I could do together when she gets a little stronger."

"I noticed how frail she seems. Addiction can weaken a person's overall health quickly. Walking and running would be a good beginning exercise for her. That time on the beach will heal her soul, too."

"Exactly. This is delicious, Randy." Jenn took another bite. "There's something unusual about the sauce. It's very tasty. I can't figure out what all the ingredients are."

"That's a well-guarded secret, my dear." Randy winked.

"I don't suppose I need to know as long as you will keep making it." Jenn continued chewing. "Speaking of soul healing, how do you think Joe is doing in that regard?"

"Joe is jumping back into his job with both feet. That may be one of the best things he can do, at this point, to help himself heal. One of the hardest obstacles for him to deal with is going to be what happens to Samantha Fairfield. Based on the evidence as I know it now, I don't think there is any doubt that she will serve some time for this crime. No matter how Joe feels about her as time goes on, she is still the woman who raised him. She is the mother of Joe the child. The adult version now has an opportunity to have another set of parents. I doubt that he can completely let go of Samantha without some strong grief."

"Renee and I have discussed that several times since his return. Renee wishes that the woman didn't know that Joe was kidnapped. She feels a great deal of gratitude to the woman because of the love and care she obviously gave Joe. Then, she remembers that Samantha basically told Woodrow to go get her a child and that knowledge cancels out any good feelings Renee has toward her. Would the sentence be such that Samantha would spend the rest of her life in prison?"

"I would imagine so. Any judge will make the punishment stiff, especially because of all the time that Samantha could have tried to rectify the situation. The judge will want to send a message that clearly shows that a crime against a child will be severely punished. I don't have any knowledge if Joe has tried to make any contact with Samantha so far. You know, I was there when she was arrested. Joe insisted on standing in the room while Samantha was read her rights. There wasn't any interaction between them after that moment. I wondered at the time if I was witnessing their goodbye."

"Oh, Randy, for all the happiness I have felt for Renee and Neil, I've thought about that it isn't completely happy for Joe. He's going to have a wonderful new life here in Serendipity with a family who has so much love to give him. But it's like the last twenty years were a lie. From what Joe has revealed, his childhood was not too happy. All that moving around that he's spoken of is enough to make his childhood memories lonely and sad."

"You're right. Joe has told me quite a bit about those years. I don't think he had any real stability until he was in high school. I believe he formed a few friendships and made a couple of special bonds with some teachers. Samantha Fairfield has been the real constant in his life. Now he's learned that she wasn't truthful either. I'd be concerned about Joe's ability to form relationships if I didn't see him seemingly already developing some strong bonds with a couple of people. Joe's quickly becoming tight with Foster. I also think that his relationship with Megan is falling right back into place."

"I think it's going to take time for a closeness with Renee and Neil to form. For some reason, it's extra awkward for each of them." Jenn took a bite of salad. "I'm happy to hear that he's bonding with Foster. That will be good for them both. Everyone is glad that Joe has you in his life."

Randy watched Jenn continuing to enjoy the food. Something about the moment reminded him of eating dinner at the Halston house while they were growing up. Randy remembered wishing that he and Jenn would someday share dinner every night. His wish hadn't come true. Yet. For the first time in his life, he could see that becoming a reality though. *I could get used to this.*

"Davenport, you don't have to hover outside my doorway. Either come in or move on."

Randy shook his head in amusement. The young man had lived in Randy's house, but he was afraid to knock on his office door.

"I'm sorry. I don't want to bother you." Joe stepped through the doorway into the office.

"I don't ever use the word 'bother' in reference to my team or the people we serve. That covers everyone within a good size radius of me. What's on your mind, Joe?"

"I had the strangest thing happen to me this morning, Chief." Joe stood in front of Randy's desk.

"Considering what I know about your life, I'm anxious to hear this, or maybe I'm not." Randy raised an eyebrow.

"I was doing some patrolling downtown. Captain Crockett mentioned to me about the situation with the children leaving handprints on the windows at that sewing store near the Visitors Bureau."

"Sew What."

"Well, I thought that was something you wanted us to keep an eye on." Joe frowned. "I believe there was a complaint from the owner."

Randy laughed, shaking his head. "I wasn't challenging you. The name of the store is Sew What."

"Oh, yeah, I forgot." Joe grinned. "Anyway, I stopped in there to ask the owner if she had found anymore handprints on the front window or door. I believe her name is Miss Lowe."

"Yes, that would be Amelia. She and I went to school together. Her mother was something else. All the little boys feared Mrs. Lowe. I'm the one who took the complaint from Amelia. We watched the business for several nights and discovered that a couple of kids thought it was fun to leave their fingerprints. Captain Crockett went down there the next night and asked the boys if they'd like to give us their fingerprints. I doubt they've been back."

"I guess the Captain got their attention. Miss Lowe was quite happy that her windows have been remaining clean. She sends her thanks."

"Was that the strange thing that happened?"

"No, sir. It was what happened after I left the store. I was walking down the street back to my patrol car and I was approached by a man. What I found strange about our conversation, or maybe I should call it coincidental, was that the man was looking for a lost relative."

"You've got to be joking." Randy shook his head. "This is Serendipity though—the land of happy accidents."

"Nope. I couldn't make this up if I tried. I was concerned at first because I was afraid that someone had become lost or, heaven forbid, had been abducted."

"Good grief."

"That wasn't the case. The man was looking for a relative that he really didn't know but was trying to find."

"Well, I assume that person must have some connection to our town. Did he tell you the person's name?"

"No, he seemed hesitant to do that. I don't know why. He asked me if I could direct him to the local library and to the newspaper office."

"I could see where the library might have some records he could use, but why the newspaper office?"

"I asked him that. He said that he thought he might search the obituaries to see if the person was dead."

"I'll agree that was a strange conversation. You, of all people, being the officer he approached. If he only knew your story. It's also strange that he's searching the obituaries. I would think that would be the last place he'd want to find who he was looking for."

"I know. Like I said, it was strange, all around. I enjoyed it though. I'm enjoying every day."

Joe's radio went off, summoning him to a call. He nodded at Randy before leaving the room.

"I wonder who in the world that man was looking for." Randy chuckled. "Maybe I should alert Jenn since she's so good at detective work. The way things have been going, Jenn probably knows who the man is looking for."

CHAPTER THREE

Doris

THE DING OF THE bell that hung on the front door took Doris' attention away from the email she was reading. Walking toward her desk was a man who appeared to be in his late fifties, a little salt and pepper in his hair, a tall athletic build making his strides long.

"Good afternoon, sir, how may I help you?" Doris rose from her chair, pulling down the blouse of her bright coral polyester pantsuit. Doris always stood up when a customer entered the building, a gesture of respect.

"Good afternoon. I am visiting the area doing some genealogy research. I'm wondering if you have access to past editions of your newspapers."

"We do not have many bound issues any longer, that has been replaced by technology. We do have digital copies of every issue back to the inception of this newspaper in the early 1900s."

"That's impressive. I do not need to go back too far in my search. I'm trying to find my birth mother. First on my list is to determine if she is still living. I thought I could peruse your obituary section for the past few years and hope that I do not find her name there."

"Have you considered doing an internet search for the name to see if you can find an obituary online? That would be quicker than looking through years of obituary sections."

"I had not thought of that. It would be quicker. Thank you for that good idea. I will go back to my hotel and begin searching." The man smiled, turning to walk away.

"I don't mean to be intrusive." Doris leaned over the counter. "I have lived in Serendipity all my life. I might know the lady you are searching for, if you would like to share her name."

The man came back to the counter. He tilted his head, looking at Doris. She wondered if he was sizing her up, deciding if he could trust her.

"I don't want to invade this woman's privacy. The adoption was private. I found my original birth certificate in some of my family's papers. As you can see from the gray in this hair, it happened a long time ago." The man took a deep breath. "My birth mother was not a teenager. She was in her mid-twenties. I suppose it is possible that it wasn't even a secret. I was not born here, but the record showed that this town was her place of residence."

"I see that you are wrestling with yourself. I should not have asked such a personal question. Forgive me."

A smile crossed the man's lips. He laid his notebook on the counter, extending his hand.

"My name is Ross Lancaster."

"It's nice to meet you, Mr. Lancaster. My name is Doris Hudson."

"Please call me Ross."

"You must call me Doris then."

"Doris, I'm going to tell you the name of the woman I am searching for. You seem like the trustworthy sort."

Ross smiled broadly. She was struck by something familiar. Doris had seen that smile before. Her mind raced through her memory. It was a long time ago. She could almost see the person. Ross' voice brought her back from the past.

"I'm sorry, Ross. My mind wandered momentarily. It happens with age. What did you say?"

"I said that my birth mother's name was Rachel Frederick."

Doris gasped. Quickly, she covered her mouth with her hand. She knew who the person was who had that same smile. His name was Jordan Rivers. The man who broke her best friend's heart.

"Sometimes I think about selling this old house. It's too big for me to ramble around during my final years. It's probably selfish of me to keep it. I could leave it to one of Paisley's daughters, since I don't have anyone to directly inherit it."

Rachel poured Doris a glass of iced tea. Swirling in Doris' mind were the words she needed to say to Rachel. *Sometimes friends need to say hard words.* Doris took a drink of her tea.

"You seem preoccupied, Doris. Did you hear any juicy gossip at the newspaper today?"

Doris gave Rachel a wide-eyed look, shocked at how spot-on Rachel's comment was.

"We call it news, Rachel." Doris stalled for time. Her mind hadn't worked out the words yet.

"One person's news is another's gossip. It all depends on motive." Rachel stared at Doris. "You seem so tense. What in the world happened today that has you on edge?"

"Rachel, I do have something to tell you. It's not going to be easy for you to hear."

"Doris Hudson, don't you dare scare me. You didn't have a doctor's appointment today that you forgot to tell me about. I cannot have my best friend dying of something. We haven't gone on our Mediterranean cruise yet." Rachel's expression became sad and serious.

"Stop jumping to conclusions. I did not go to the doctor today. I'm healthy as a horse." Doris took a deep breath. "But something surprising happened. I met someone who I never imagined I would meet."

"That sounds exciting. I'm very curious. Who could it possibly be? Was it someone important?"

Rachel's eyes darted from side-to-side. Doris could see her friend's anxious curiosity.

"Isn't everyone important?"

"You are right. That was a shallow statement on my part. Was it someone interesting? That's a fair question, isn't it?"

"The person was quite interesting. The person is on a mission of discovery. He's searching for his family."

"Goodness. Is his family lost? This is reminding me of our dear lost Jonah. Who I've got to get used to calling Joe." Rachel frowned. "A lost child is a tragic thing."

The irony of Rachel's words did not escape Doris. The thought brought a tear to Doris' eye. She briefly turned away.

"The man's family is not lost exactly. But he hasn't had the opportunity to know them."

"I'm sure his family will be thrilled to meet him. Were you able to help him with his search?"

"I have not helped him yet, but I could do so. I must ask someone's permission first."

"Permission? I don't understand. I would think that helping anyone is part of your job at the newspaper."

"It really doesn't have to do with the newspaper, Rachel. The man's journey is a personal one. He's searching for his birth mother."

Silence hung between Doris and Rachel. The two women had been friends for the better portion of their lives. There were not many secrets left untold, except one that Rachel never seemed to want to talk about. Doris knew the outside of the story. Even she did not know the heart of it.

"The man's name is Ross Lancaster. He is looking for Rachel Frederick. He has Jordan Rivers' smile."

"I thought this day might eventually come." Rachel took a long, deep breath, before looking down, twirling a ring on her right hand. "I expected it to occur sooner though. He's sixty years old now."

"Yes, his hair is salt and pepper."

"Does he look like Jordan?"

"Only when he smiles. Of course, I only saw one photograph of Jordan, and he was certainly much younger in the photo than the man is I met today. Do you have any idea if Jordan is still living?"

"I lost track of him years ago. I doubt he is still living. Jordan was over a dozen years older than me. He would be in his late nineties now."

"You've never talked about him or what happened between you."

"In the beginning, I was ashamed. As the years passed, it was easier not to talk about him, easier not to remember."

"Ashamed? Of the pregnancy?"

"Yes. But mostly ashamed of the fact that he was a married man."

"I don't remember you telling me he was married. I believe you only said that it didn't work out between you."

"You and I barely knew each other then, Doris. Our age difference doesn't seem like much now. I am eighty-five and you are seventy-eight. Seven years seems barely a difference. Back then, the gap was greater. I was twenty-five, you were eighteen. I was a woman. You were a girl."

"And, yet, we became friends."

"You discovered my secret and did not turn away. You kept my secret and became my dearest friend."

"It has not been hard. We are kindred spirits, you and I." Doris reached over and squeezed Rachel's hand. "Do you think you would like to meet your son?"

Doris watched Rachel's face. A world of emotions crossed her expression. Rachel's eyes glistened with tears that soon escaped, gently rolling down her checks.

"I would love to meet him. I can't imagine why he would want to meet the person who gave him away."

"I know nothing about him other than what I gleaned from our brief encounter. He seems like a fine man. That must have something to do with a good upbringing, hopefully in a loving home. If he is looking for you, that means he has some appreciation for that."

"Do you really think so?"

"The biggest concern that I heard today was that he would find out you were deceased. I did not reveal whether you were or not. I asked him if I could have his phone number. I said that I would try to do some research to help him."

"Oh, that was smart. Thank you, Doris."

"I'm keeping your secret, Rachel. Remember though, you are quite well-known in this community. He might ask others."

"Yes. I will not let this opportunity pass me by. I want to meet him, if he wants to meet me. I've got to prepare myself though. It's been a long time."

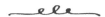

"Thank you for meeting me, Ross."

Doris sat across from Ross Lancaster at Quincy's Diner the following morning. The man looked anxious.

"I didn't expect to hear from you so soon. I'm afraid that might mean that what I first suspected was true. Is Rachel Frederick deceased?"

"No, Ross. Not at all, Rachel is very much alive. I had dinner with her last evening."

"What?" Ross was visibly shocked. "How did you find her so quickly?"

"Rachel Frederick has been my best friend for most of my adult life."

"Why didn't you tell me that yesterday?" Ross furrowed his brow.

"Because Rachel is my friend and I need to protect her. I wanted her to be prepared for the possibility of meeting you before I told you. I had to make sure she was okay with the idea."

"I understand. That means you are a loyal friend." Ross took a deep breath. "Since you have contacted me, does that mean she is willing to see me?"

Doris saw an eagerness, with a touch of fear, in the man's face. It gave a hint of what a younger version of him might have looked like.

"It does. First, however, you and I are going to have a little chat."

"I never expected this quest I have been on to be this easy."

"Tell me what has caused you to take this journey."

"From a young age, I knew that I was adopted. In my family, it was talked about so normally, that I remember asking my friends in elementary school if they were adopted." Ross chuckled. "That caused my teacher some issues with having to explain what that meant. My parents were called to the principal's office the next day when so many parents complained about their children coming home from school asking if they were adopted."

"What grade were you in when that occurred?"

"Second grade, about seven years old."

"Oh, my goodness, that must have created quite a stir."

"Yes, it certainly did. As I said, my adoption was treated as something ordinary in my house. I was an only child. My father died about thirty years ago. My mother asked me once if I wanted to try and find my birth parents. It wasn't something that seemed important to me until my mother passed away about a year ago. During the weeks and months after her death as I went through her things, I found my original birth certificate. The birth certificate I have used for most of my life has my adoptive parents listed. I was surprised that my parents had a copy of the original one. It was in my parents' fire safe box underneath their marriage certificate. That's how I found out my birth mother's name."

"Was your birth father listed?"

"No. Do you know who he is?"

"I do, Ross. That is not information for me to tell though; that should come from Rachel."

"I understand. Is she in good health? I'm thinking that she must be in her mid-eighties."

"Rachel is fit as a fiddle. She has some issues with mobility, mainly because of arthritis. Overall, her health is excellent."

"Are you sure she is willing to meet me? Through the years, I've known many others who were adopted. One lady that I worked with found her birth mother. The woman was willing to meet my friend. She was not willing to introduce her daughter to the family she created after her. My friend was heartbroken. That's one of the reasons I've never searched until now."

"Absolutely, Rachel is thrilled with the idea. She's also quite nervous and a little scared."

"Why is she scared?"

"She gave you up. Mothers don't normally do that. A child might not understand."

"My adopted mother told me several times while I was growing up that my birth mother must have had an important reason as to why she gave me up. That she must have thought someone else could give me a better life. Since I found my original birth certificate and saw my mother's age, I've wondered about that. Rachel Frederick was almost twenty-five when I was born. It wasn't like she was a teenager."

"I'm sure you've discovered this by now, Ross. Life is complicated. Things aren't always as they seem. There can be underlying reasons or circumstances which force us to make difficult decisions. Rachel's reasons need to be explained by her." Doris checked the time on her phone. "How long do you plan to stay in the area, Ross?"

"I don't have a specific time in mind. I'm retired, so I am not tied to a work schedule. I imagined that I would be here a couple of days. When do you think Rachel will be willing to see me?"

"If you are ready, the day is today."

Chapter Four

Rachel

Every woman has a box of secrets. No matter how old or young, there are special items tucked away which tell a version of her life which most people never know. The box may get bigger or smaller as the decades pass, but the box always exists.

Rachel imagined that one day her nieces would find her box. They would comb through the contents, speculating on how old Rachel had been when she wore the red ribbon they found or who gave her the jeweled hair comb with the butterfly on it. The girls would giggle at the photo of Rachel and her sister Paisley as toddlers sitting in an old wash tub with soap in their hair. They wouldn't know that the green marble had belonged to a brother who died of pneumonia when he was only seven. No one would recognize the two men in separate black and white photos in the bottom of the box. One photo was of a man who died too young. The other one was a newspaper clipping about the father of the man who was following Doris down Rachel's front sidewalk.

Taking a deep breath, Rachel straightened her posture in the blue recliner where she always sat in the living room. Getting up and down was difficult for her arthritic legs. Knowing that, Doris would let herself and the man in. Rachel's hands trembled. There was nothing normally wrong with her hands. The trembling was caused by the meeting that was about to occur. It was sixty years in the making. Rachel was terrified.

"Rachel, we're here." Doris' friendly voice carried easily in the high-ceiling house.

It was the first house that Carson Frederick built for his devoted wife, Elana. Given to their oldest daughter when Carson and Elana moved to the oceanfront property Carson built, the never married Rachel lived her entire life in the home. It was too big for one person and too expensive to heat. Yet, Rachel could not imagine living anywhere else.

"I'm in the living room, Doris." Rachel closed her eyes, thinking a silent prayer.

Doris appeared in the doorway. Her smile was bright. Seconds later, a man was standing behind Doris. Rachel could not contain the gasp which escaped her mouth. Doris told her that the only resemblance was in the man's smile. Rachel did not agree. To her, it was as if Jordan Rivers was standing in her living room, in the same spot where Jordan endured a tongue-lashing from her father during his one-and-only visit to the house.

Rachel quickly covered her mouth, trying to regain her composure. It was difficult to do when you were time-travelling.

"Rachel, this is Ross Lancaster." Doris extended her hand for the man to enter the expansive room. "Ross, this is Rachel Frederick."

Slowly, the man walked toward her. His stride was confident, yet cautious. Rachel could only imagine the multiple thoughts running through this man's head. Her own thoughts were a mixture of wonder, amazement, and regret. Every time, through the years, when Rachel allowed herself to briefly imagine this meeting, she saw a young boy running toward her. Never did she see a retired man with gray in his hair. Time could be cruel. Rachel did not know what she ate for breakfast yesterday. She could still smell a newborn she held only for a few precious moments sixty years ago. *How could that child possibly be this man?*

"I'm pleased to meet you, ma'am." The man walked toward her, extending his hand in greeting.

Rachel reached out, gently taking hold of the man's hand. His touch was gentle. She was flooded with the memory of Jordan taking the same hand to help her out of his car the first time they met. The encounter seemed innocent enough. She was visiting an aunt a couple of hundred miles away from Serendipity. The aunt asked her neighbor to pick Rachel up at the train station on his way home from work. During the drive to her aunt's home, Jordan became infatuated with the young Rachel. And, Rachel, she fell hopelessly in love.

"Thank you for agreeing to see me."

Ross Lancaster released Rachel's hand, jarring her back into the present.

"Certainly." Rachel's hand returned to her lap. She could still feel Ross' touch. *Or was it the memory of Jordan's?* "Doris tells me that you live in Richmond, Virginia. Have you always lived there?"

Small talk. A proper Southern lady could make polite small talk in any situation. Elana Frederick engrained this into her daughters.

"No. I grew up in a suburb of Washington, D.C. My father worked for the Smithsonian. I moved to Richmond when my wife and I got married, after college."

"Married? Did your wife come with you?" Rachel had not considered that this man would be married. He probably had children. *Her grandchildren. Oh, my goodness.*

"My wife passed away ten years ago from cancer."

"Oh, I'm so sorry." Rachel felt a deep sadness overcome her. Was it possible that she could feel his grief?

"We had twenty-five wonderful years together. Her illness took her quickly. I am thankful that she did not suffer."

"I imagine that you two have much to talk about." Doris was still standing in the doorway. "If you don't need me for anything, Rachel, I'm going to head on into work."

"The newspaper cannot survive long without its nucleus." Rachel smiled at her friend. "I appreciate you bringing Mr. Lancaster here. Have a good day."

"Thank you, Doris." Ross walked over to Doris, extending his hand. "I appreciate your help. It was a pleasure to meet you."

After Doris left, Rachel motioned for Ross to sit down across from her. She took a deep breath anticipating all the questions her biological son would have for her.

"Before you begin your questions, I'd like to tell you that I am truly happy that you have found me and chosen to visit. There's not been a day since you were born that I have not thought about you and wondered how you were. When you give a child up for adoption, you also give up the right to seek them out later. It doesn't lessen your desire to do so though."

"You probably wonder why I have not looked for you sooner. I always knew that I was adopted. I did not know that there was a document in my parents' possession that would tell me who you were. Since it was a private adoption, there are not any public records. My public birth certificate lists my adoptive parents and my current legal name. It wasn't until after my mother passed and I was going through her belongings that I found my original birth certificate in the bottom of a secure box with other papers. I wonder if she also had forgotten of its existence."

"It's been a long time ago."

"I would like to hear your story, if you are willing to share it. My parents did not reveal any details about you. I assume they knew none. You are the only person who could tell me who my biological father is or was."

"I will certainly tell you. It is your story as much as it is mine. Help yourself to a glass of tea, if you like. This will take a little while."

"I'm anxious to hear about your life."

Rachel looked away from Ross, staring out the window that was next to her chair. She would be time-travelling again, far back to a time she rarely allowed herself to visit. It was a turning point in her life.

"I was the oldest child of Carson and Elana Frederick. My father was a successful carpenter who built the largest construction company in the eastern part of this state. The company still exists. It's now run by my niece's husband."

Ross poured himself a glass of the iced tea she prepared that morning. An almost full glass of the beverage already sat on the table beside her chair.

"Both my sister and I were raised in this house that our father built himself before we were born. We were sent to college and became educated young women in a time when most girls were expected to marry as soon as possible and become housewives and mothers. I decided to become a teacher because having summers off was quite attractive to me. My sister majored in business. After college, I quickly secured a teaching position in a neighboring county. After a couple of years of teaching, I began taking night classes to pursue a graduate degree in the hopes of getting into school administration."

"Education is the cornerstone of our society. One of the most noble professions there is."

Ross gently placed the glass of tea on a coaster on the table beside him. The glint of light coming in through the window behind him made the amber color of tea gleam like sunlight.

"It has been my life's work." Rachel took a sip of her drink. "The summer before you were born, I spent a month with my Aunt Ardelia in a small town on the coast of South Carolina. My Uncle Henry had passed a few months earlier and my aunt wanted some company. I took the train from Raleigh to Charleston. My aunt's neighbor was a businessman who worked in Charleston every day. She asked him to pick me up at the train station."

Rachel's phone buzzed. Picking it up, she saw that the call was from Renee. Rachel thought of the son who had so cruelly been taken from her niece and the joy of their reunion twenty years later. She let the call go to voicemail, wondering to herself if she would tell her nieces about their cousin.

"It was a little over an hour's drive from Charleston to Aunt Ardelia's house. The man and I had a lively conversation. He was in his late thirties. A lawyer working in a successful practice. He was a junior partner in the firm. The man was different from anyone I had ever met. He had a wicked sense of humor. The young men I had dated up until that point seemed so one-dimensional to me. They lacked depth and conviction, content to converse about the sports of the day but never knowing the news of the world. I found those conversations stale and predictable. This man was different. By the time we reached the driveway that he shared with my aunt's home, I was quite enamored with the man. A gentleman, he opened my door, taking my hand to help me out of his car. For a moment just now, when you took my hand in introduction, I was reminded of that moment. Your touch is gentle, as was his."

"Was this man my father?"

"Yes, he was. His name was Jordan Rivers, the love of my life."

"His name was not listed on the birth certificate. Is there a reason why?"

Rachel furrowed her brow. This would begin the parts of the story that made it complicated. Layers and layers of circumstances that by themselves might have led to a different outcome. Combined, there seemed to be no choice, at the time.

"Jordan was married when I met him. He was a dozen years older than me, and he was married." Rachel heard the repetition in her words. It was their biggest obstacle.

"I see. That must have complicated the relationship."

"Indeed. It was complicated from start to finish. Now that you know a portion of the circumstances, do you want to hear the whole story?"

"I do. It's the core of the reason I came."

"Then hear it, you shall. Sit back and make yourself comfortable."

Rachel spent the next few minutes recounting the car ride from the train station and the conversation between two strangers. Rachel would admit that at eighty-five, her memory did have a few holes. She had not forgotten her time with Jordan though. Her memory of their time together was perfectly intact. So vivid were her recollections that it would often seem like she was travelling back to that time, decades ago.

"It must have been quite unusual for two strangers with such an age difference to converse so comfortably." Ross spoke when Rachel paused in her story.

"From the moment the car door closed until we reached my aunt's house, Jordan and I never stopped talking. It was as if we'd known each other for years. The rhythm of our dialogue was like old friends conversing."

"Was that where the attraction between you began or was it more physical?"

Rachel was a little surprised at the directness and depth of Ross' question. She supposed though that if you'd waited your whole life, in his case sixty years, to find out about the people who caused your birth, it would not seem personal to be so blunt.

"I might have answered that question differently at that time. Like you, Jordan was quite handsome. From this vantage point of age and experience, I would certainly surmise that our attraction was born from a comfortable and instant connection. It was like we had known each other and were being reunited. We were finishing each other's sentences. That is not an exaggeration."

"But he was married. That was a roadblock."

"I was not aware that Jordan was married until we arrived at my aunt's house. He never mentioned his wife. My aunt did not mention her until dinner that evening. I was in shock because, by that point, Jordan had already invited to show me around Charleston the following day."

"That does seem strange with a wife right next door."

"Oh, Mrs. Rivers was not living with Jordan at the time. That was another complication. She was staying in a sanitarium in Charleston and had been there for almost a year at that point."

"What was wrong with the woman?"

"Mrs. Rivers had several miscarriages. Jordan did not tell me much about her. Aunt Ardelia, however, told me her story in detail. The failed pregnancies left her in a fragile mental state. I do not believe that Jordan wanted her to be hospitalized, but her parents pressed the matter. Apparently, there was a history of mental illness in the woman's extended family with suicide as an outcome."

"Her parents feared the worst."

"I suppose so. The little that Jordan shared with me about his wife later gave me the impression that rather than get better, her mental state had deteriorated further while in the sanitarium. He did not think she would recover. He was planning to divorce her." Rachel took a deep breath. "I suppose that I naively felt sorry for Jordan. He seemed to enjoy my company. I could turn his look of forlorn into a smile. I honestly didn't intentionally set out to have an affair with him. But I was drawn to him like a moth to a flame. I longed to be in his company. I did not possess the power to stop myself."

"I suppose that I should be thankful that you did not. My existence hinged on this encounter." Ross smiled. His expression appeared to be full of understanding. There was no judgment in his eyes, Jordan's eyes.

"Days turned into weeks. I saw Jordan daily. If my aunt knew what was going on, she did not let on. Thinking back over the years, I don't believe that Aunt Ardelia imagined our behavior was possible for either one of us. Tours of Charleston were followed by long evenings of conversations in the backyards of the adjacent homes. Those trips into the city included dinners at nice restaurants with entertainment at theaters or dancing in nightclubs. I looked a little older than my age. He had youthful movie star looks. To strangers who encountered us, we probably appeared like any other couple dating. Jordan was a gentleman. He was never more physical than taking my hand to help me out of the car or placing his hand on the small of my back to lead me in front of him."

"That had to change at some point. I believe I am living proof of something far more physical transpiring."

Ross laughed, a hearty chuckle. Rachel clutched her heart.

"Are you okay?" Ross' tone quickly changed to one of concern.

"Your laugh, it is just like your father's. It shocks my heart to hear the sound after all these years. Jordan's laugh was like music to my ears."

"My wife used to say that I laughed like someone who thought their jokes were funny."

"That's an interesting way to put it. I would agree with her description though. Jordan found humor in what he was saying before he finished his sentences." Rachel relaxed a moment, taking a sip of her tea, listening to the tick of the mantle clock. "I blame Aunt Ardelia for my relationship with Jordan becoming a physical one."

"That must be an interesting turn in this story."

"My visit was three months long. Around the beginning of the third month, Aunt Ardelia took a short trip to attend the funeral of her late husband's sister. She was gone for four days. Those are four days I will never forget."

"I don't suppose that most children hear the impassioned story of their conception. Why don't we skip those details, and you give me a more G-rated version? I don't want to dream about it later."

There it was again—Jordan's humor. It was amazing.

"The abbreviated version is that as fate would have it, Jordan had an unpleasant visit with his wife at the hospital the same day my aunt departed on her trip. Later that evening, I found him sitting on his back porch with a half-drunk bottle of scotch. According to Jordan, his wife had a violent outburst during the visit, thrashing at him, telling him that she wanted to die. He was shaken and upset upon his return home. Jordan tried to drown his sorrows in that bottle. He was quite drunk when I found him, crying drunk, inconsolable. One thing led to another. At some point during those four days, you were conceived."

"Before I found my birth certificate and saw your age, I imagined my adoption resulted because of an unplanned teenage pregnancy. Most adoption stories seem to begin that way. I'm shocked to learn that my biological parents were both adults. There must be more to this love story."

"There are more twists without a happy ending, except that a beautiful baby boy came into the world. Despite my regrets, I believe I now can assume that I gave you a happy beginning and a good life by giving you up."

"You did. With no disrespect intended, I cannot imagine having two better parents than I did or a happier upbringing. I was loved unconditionally. It has made the loss of my parents almost unbearable, their love for me was so strong."

"That is a blessing to this old woman's heart. That is a true blessing. This knowledge will give me the strength to tell you the rest of this story. My story. Jordan's story. Your story."

Just then, Ross' cell phone rang. Taking it from a holder on his belt, Ross stood up when he saw the screen.

"Excuse me. I need to take this. It's my daughter."

Rachel nodded and Ross left the room, walking into the foyer of the house.

His daughter. My granddaughter. Dare she allow herself to think that way? Was it possible for a woman of eight-five years to become a first-time mother and grandmother? Her heart sped up at the thought. Sensing that the phone call might take a few minutes, Rachel rose from her chair and made her way to the bathroom. When she returned, she found Ross sitting on the couch.

"I hope everything is okay." Rachel sat in her chair.

"It is. My daughter was checking on me. I told her that I was going out of town for a few days."

"May I ask about your family?"

"Certainly. It's one of my favorite topics."

Ross' broad smile showed his pride. Pulling his phone out of its holster again, Ross scrolled on the screen for a few moments before handing the phone to Rachel.

"This is my favorite photo of my family. It was taken about a year before my wife passed away. Our son and daughter were younger then. They are both adults now. Neither of them has married yet."

"Ross, what a beautiful family. What was your wife's name?"

"Aretta. Our children are Elijah and Ruth."

"Beautiful. Those are Biblical names."

"Aretta had a strong faith. She sought names for our children from her favorite book."

"I imagine that faith was both put to the test during her illness and a source of great strength for her." Rachel handed the phone back to Ross.

"You are exactly right." Ross looked at the photo again before putting the phone away. "Please continue with your story. What happened when your aunt returned from her trip?"

"Aunt Ardelia returned and the four days that Jordan and I had together were over. He went back to work in Charleston. He told me that he would be staying overnight to talk more extensively to his wife's doctors. When he came back that weekend, Jordan seemed different, preoccupied. He apologized about what happened between us. He said that he shouldn't have taken advantage of the situation."

"How did you feel about it?"

Rachel stared at Ross for a moment. He asked good questions. She could hear empathy in his tone. She could see the same in his expression. Rachel said a silent word of thanks to his parents, the Lancasters, for taking such care in raising her son, their son.

"As you know, I was not a schoolgirl. I was a young woman in my mid-twenties. While I certainly didn't have vast experience in the adult world, I, also, wasn't totally naïve. I can't say for a certainty, but I do not think I would have allowed the relationship to progress to the point it did, had it not been that Mrs. Rivers was seemingly in a mental state that she would never recover from. Somewhere deep inside, I believed that Jordan would soon be free of the marriage, and we would be together."

"Since I did not grow up in a home with you and Jordan, I presume that did not happen."

Ross' blunt statement caught Rachel off-guard. He was certainly speaking the truth. It stunned her for a moment.

"No, it did not. What happened was quite the contrary. During the following couple of weeks, Jordan spent more nights in Charleston than he did at his home. Knowing that I would soon be returning to my home, I tried to start putting him out of my mind. Jordan was not available to drive me back to the train station on the day I went home."

Overcome with emotion, Rachel stopped talking for a moment. Ross sat in silence while she retrieved a handkerchief that was tucked into the sleeve of her blouse and dried her eyes.

"It was like a scene out of an old black and white movie. I was sitting in my seat on the train, next to the window. As the train began to pull away from the station, I saw Jordan standing on the platform. Our eyes met. Tears streamed down my face. He raised his hand and blew me a kiss. I turned around in my seat and waved until I could no longer see him."

"He came to see you off. He cared."

"That probably would have been the end to this story had it not been that about two weeks after I returned home, I began throwing up every morning. I went to the doctor, naively thinking that I had a stomach bug. My melancholy state did not give me much of an appetite. I couldn't imagine why I was sick. I was shocked to hear the real reason."

"Were you living here with your parents?"

"Yes. My parents were quite loving and supportive, but I knew this news would not be a happy topic in my family. I decided that before I revealed anything to them, I would tell Jordan."

"Were you hoping that he would marry you?"

"Even though I knew that would be complicated, that was my silent hope. I knew that it would seem strange for me to travel back there so soon. It was time for school to start. I needed to be in my classroom. I called him at his office. Jordan sounded happy to hear from me. There was a long silence when I revealed my reason for calling. I called him on a Wednesday morning. He said that he would travel to Serendipity on Saturday. Those were the three longest days of my life."

"It was a different time then. Everything took longer, didn't it? Technology changed some of that."

"I suppose you are right. Travel was different as well. I'm not sure what could have made those days shorter for me though. I was full of a mixture of excitement and dread. It was a painful combination."

"I wonder if I felt that." Ross tilted his head, looking off into space.

"I suppose that is possible on some level. You were mighty small at that point."

Rachel heard a siren. Looking out her window, she saw a rescue squad pass.

"I had offered to meet Jordan at the train station in Raleigh. He declined my offer, saying that he would find a way to Serendipity. I stood guard by the phone Saturday morning, daring anyone to even get close to it. No one knew why I was behaving so strangely. I had not dared to breathe a word about Jordan since I returned home. I had no reason to think that Aunt Ardelia had mentioned Jordan to my parents, other than him being her nice neighbor who picked me up at the train station. Aunt Ardelia knew little about my meetings with Jordan. I told her that I met some young people in her town who I was spending some of my evenings with. I learned later that she knew far more than I realized."

"Older folks are more observant than we give them credit for. I've learned that since I've become one of them."

Rachel heard Jordan's laugh again. This time, it pained her heart.

"Jordan finally called. I met him at a park near the library. He was sitting on a bench when I arrived. He looked a decade older than his years, like he hadn't slept. His smile was forced. I told him the basic details of being sick and going to the doctor. We sat in silence for a few moments. We each seemed to be waiting for the other one to speak. When Jordan finally spoke, he told me that he'd talked to a lawyer friend of his from another firm who specialized in adoptions. He said that we could easily find a couple who wanted a child. A couple who could not have a child, but desperately wanted one. I sat there stunned, not believing what I was hearing."

"Adoption wasn't your idea?" Ross seemed surprised.

"No. The thought had never crossed my mind. I figured that I would have the baby and raise it. The idea was still fresh in my mind. I don't think I ever considered that Jordan wouldn't be a part of that equation."

"I see."

"I told him that. Jordan kept shaking his head and saying 'no.' I pressed him further. Finally, he revealed the information that would change everything. During those weeks before our four days together, the doctors had begun a new treatment regimen on Jordan's wife. They gave her a medicine which hadn't been tried on her before. At first, she had a strange reaction to the meds. It appeared to make her condition worse. The doctors adjusted the dosage. She began to respond to it. A month or so before the new treatment began, Jordan and his wife had a conjugal visit at the hospital. She was pregnant. Things were going well with this pregnancy. His wife's mental state was almost back to normal. It was a miracle. He had to take care of his wife and child."

"Only one child." Ross took a deep breath, then exhaled.

"Only one wife." Rachel felt old anger rise in her. It was combined with the pain she saw on Ross' face. "The rest of that day went by in a blur. I don't have a clear memory in my mind. I spent the bulk of it crying, angry at everyone. Jordan accompanied me back to this house. To his credit, he faced the wrath of my father, in this very room. He told my parents the story of how our relationship transpired. Jordan took all the blame, saying that he should have not taken advantage of me. He told them the story of his wife, the children they had lost, her mental state, and how things had changed."

"How did your parents react?"

"Like me, my mother sat there and cried. I never felt shame from either of them. I think she was more afraid than anything. Afraid of how my life would turn out. My strong but mild-mannered father was angry. He probably could have killed Jordan with his bare hands. Even though I saw pain cross his face when Jordan brought up adoption, I could see the businessman in him thinking that it was the most rational choice. He kept telling me to 'think of the child,' that so many couples wanted children and would give the baby a loving home with two parents, not one. He glared at Jordan with those words."

"Your father was not wrong. I will say again, I had a wonderful childhood. My parents were those people your father was talking about. They tried to have children for over ten years before my father's college roommate called him one night about a child that might be available to adopt. My father's friend must have been the lawyer that Jordan contacted."

"I'm thrilled to know that you had a loving upbringing with good people. I would rather your life had been spent with me. Truthfully,

I know there were too many reasons for that not to happen." Rachel frowned, shaking her head. "Jordan and my father handled the whole process after that. I went back to teaching school and was able to conceal my pregnancy until it was time for Christmas Break. I asked the school system for a leave of absence until the next school year began the following fall. Then, I packed my bags and went to stay in an apartment in Charleston that was paid for by the adoptive parents. It was an easy pregnancy. I had no medical problems at all. You were born in a hospital in Charleston. I held you for a few minutes after you were born. I left the hospital a few days later, without you. I did not meet your parents. It was better that way."

Rachel did not realize her face was covered with tears until Ross knelt in front of her.

"It's okay." Ross took hold of both of Rachel's hands. "You did a wonderful thing. You put my happiness above your own. No matter what the reasons or influence of others, it's okay. I'm happy to have the chance to meet you now and hear our story."

"Our story." Rachel smiled, squeezing Ross' hands. "It is that."

Ross released Rachel's hands, rising to go back to the couch.

"Did you ever see Jordan again?"

"I did not see or hear from him while I was staying in Charleston before your birth. While I was still in Charleston, Aunt Ardelia told my mother that the 'nice couple' next door brought home a new baby, a daughter. Aunt Ardelia was so happy that Mrs. Rivers was doing better and finally had a child to love." Rachel took a deep breath. "Again, I took the train home. Looking out the window, as the train pulled away, there was Jordan standing on the platform. This time, tears were streaming down Jordan's face. I'd cried all the tears I could by that point. My emotional well was dry. I never heard from him again. I would assume that he is probably deceased by now as he would be almost one hundred, if not."

"That's okay. I think you're the one I needed to meet."

"Do you think you would like to try to contact your sister? There could be other siblings, too."

"I don't think so. I can't imagine that she knows of my existence. It might be too shocking for her, at this point in her life."

Ross looked out the window for a few minutes. Rachel waited in silence for him to continue.

"She might want a kidney or something. That would just be awkward."

Ross laughed, this time it was more of a sarcastic cackle.

"There's my son. That comment sounds just like me."

CHAPTER FIVE

Jenn

"YOU SHOULD CHECK ON your Aunt Rachel later."

Doris spoke as Jenn passed by the front desk after returning from a mid-morning meeting.

"Is something wrong?"

"No, nothing is wrong. I'm sure she would love to hear from you though."

Jenn wondered if there was more to the story than Doris was revealing. She decided not to press further. Jenn was learning that Doris revealed what she wanted, when she wanted.

"I've taken messages for Michelle today from people in four different states. After the quiet launch of the new website for real estate and relocation, I thought it would take a while for the calls to start coming. I can already see that this is going to open a new avenue of revenue for our company." Doris handed Jenn the list of the states.

"I'm certain that we wouldn't have been able to launch this endeavor without technology. The internet has opened a world of opportunity to connect people."

"Yes, it's amazing what technology has allowed us to do as a society. You can even find people you thought were lost forever."

Jenn watched Doris' expression. Despite their conversation, Doris seemed preoccupied. Jenn wondered who or what Doris was pondering. She chose to remain silent. It was Doris' story to tell.

"I think I'll take your advice and try to call Aunt Rachel while I have a few minutes. Thanks for the reminder, Doris."

Jenn returned to her office, quickly checking her email before she attempted to call her aunt. As she expected, there were several new messages waiting for her, including one from the attorney for the Bentley estate. Jenn closed her eyes, taking a deep breath before she clicked on the email. The situation still baffled her. A chill ran down her spine thinking about the man who had so convincingly portrayed Parker Bentley. Jenn couldn't help but wonder how she would have reacted to his advances if she didn't have Randy in her life. *I am so thankful for Randy.*

The fact that she and her two sisters would now be inheriting the beautiful Bentley family home was mind-boggling. It was extra special that the mansion, aptly called the Oasis, had been built by their grandfather, Carson Frederick, for his best friend, Walter Bentley. Jenn didn't dare to go down the rabbit hole of that email. That was best left to the lawyers to manage. She needed to check on Aunt Rachel. Jenn was surprised when her aunt answered on the second ring.

"Jenn, my dear, it's wonderful to hear your voice."

"I was hoping that I would catch you. How are you doing?"

"At my age, my dear, every day on this side of the grass is a good day. I haven't been outside yet, but my day has been filled with sunshine."

Jenn pondered what Rachel said. Could the statement have something to do with why Doris suggested she check on her?

"I'm happy to hear you are having a good day."

"I've been thinking a lot about Renee today. She left a message for me earlier; I need to call her back. She's experienced so much trauma in her life. The abduction of her son and the many years of wondering what happened to him. Her cancer diagnosis and subsequent treatment. Her endurance and strength are amazing. All three of my nieces have fought their own battles in different ways. We must keep praying for Amber. She's made of tough Frederick and Halston stock. She will overcome what is plaguing her."

"Yes, she will. Renee and I are anxious for her to return from California in a few days.

"When we have the opportunity to reconnect with our loved ones, we need to embrace it as a gift."

"You sound like you've experienced that yourself. What's going on with you, Aunt Rachel?"

There was a long pause. Jenn wondered for a moment if their phone connection had been interrupted or if she'd said too much.

"When your mother left us so suddenly, Jenn, I was angry and heartbroken. I was the older one. I expected to be the first to leave. Reaching the final years of your life gives you a different perspective on the preciousness of time. Time doesn't mean as much without people you love. I know that we probably shouldn't place unequal value on people, one person meaning more than another, or one having more value in your eyes. But you will find out, if you haven't already, that there are many people throughout your life—relatives, friends, coworkers, strangers—who come and go with barely a ripple in your existence. Then, there are a few, a precious few, who take up so much room in your soul that their absence creates a literal hole in your existence and makes functioning as a normal human almost impossible. One of the worst parts is that once or twice in a lifetime, that person is someone that you never even knew was missing until you meet him or her, really meet that person, for the very first time."

"Aunt Rachel, what an amazing statement! My mind cannot completely comprehend it and yet I also perfectly understand it at the same time. Promise me that you will tell me the story behind whoever that person is to you. Don't keep that secret locked inside your heart."

Jenn's heart was full of emotion. Her mind raced in multiple directions. She thought about the precious people in her own life. She wondered who the person was that her aunt so eloquently described.

"You are certainly worthy of that knowledge. Like my sister Paisley and Doris, the sister of my heart, you and Renee are part of my soul. Soon. I will reveal it. Soon."

"Something huge happened yesterday."

Renee sat across from Jenn at Quincy's Diner for a late lunch. In the weeks since her son had been found and her cancer had miraculously gone into remission, Renee had spent most of her time in Serendipity, with a few trips to her home in Raleigh. With Neil working on a project nearby, it made sense, and offered the opportunity for both Renee and Neil to spend more time with Joe. Renee had messaged Jenn earlier that day, asking if they could meet at Quincy's when she returned from a quick visit to Raleigh.

"I'm intrigued. For you to say it is huge with the things that have happened to you lately, it must be impressive. Do tell, sis, do tell."

"Jonah, I mean Joe, try as I may, I'm still having trouble with shortening his name. While we were in Raleigh, Joe came for the day. We gave him a tour of the house, including memories of some of the things we did when he was little. When he was getting ready to head back to Serendipity, Joe called us Mom and Dad." Renee's eyes filled with tears, her voice choking. "It slipped out. He said, 'Mom and Dad, it's time for me to go.' He caught himself saying it. He frowned for a second and then a big smile crossed his face. It was like Christmas came early."

"Oh, Renee, I know that had to be a wonderful feeling for you and Neil." Jenn reached across and took both of Renee's hands in hers.

"It was like music to my ears. It came so naturally. We were so surprised. Neil and I had talked about that since he was already an adult when he was reintroduced to us, that it might be more natural for him to call us by our first names. We were okay with that. Like him being gone for twenty years, we couldn't undo it. We must accept certain things and move forward."

"That is a healthy way to view the situation. I'm sure it's not been an easy realization for you two to accept."

"It hasn't, but it's much easier than accepting that Jonah wasn't ever coming home. All those years, I couldn't accept that as the end of our family story. Now that I've gotten my wish of his return, I can accept whatever comes with it." Renee closed her eyes, a tear running down her cheek. "I'm not going to lie though, it sure felt wonderful to hear him call me Mom."

"One of the most common names in the world. Yet, it is one of the most personal." Jenn beamed with happiness for her sister. "Let's celebrate with banana splits."

"I thought the plan was to be semi-healthy with a garden salad and some French fries." Renee wiped her tears, grinning from ear to ear.

"Nope. I'm vetoing that idea. Great news is cause for a celebration. We always came to Quincy's to celebrate when we were kids. Daddy always insisted that we have banana splits. We cannot deviate from tradition."

Jenn motioned for the waitress. "We'd like two banana splits, please, and two cups of coffee."

The waitress was carrying a pot of coffee when Jenn stopped her to place the order. Since there were always coffee cups on the tables at Quincy's, the waitress filled the cups, picking up the menus off the table before she left.

Jenn's seat in the booth was facing the front door a few feet away. Looking over Renee's shoulder, Jenn saw Doris enter with a man she didn't recognize. The sound of a glass being dropped by another server at a nearby table drew Jenn's attention for a moment. When she looked back at the door, Doris and man must have been seated on the other side of restaurant as they were nowhere in sight.

While they waited for their banana splits to be made, Renee took a quick call from Neil, and Jenn checked her email. She also noticed that she had a text from Foster that only contained two words, 'Dad's coming.'

"That's a mighty big frown from someone who's about to eat like she's six instead of fifty-six."

Renee placed her phone in her purse while the waitress set the two banana splits between her and Jenn.

"Thank you." Jenn nodded at the waitress. "Foster texted that his father is coming."

"Simon's coming to Serendipity?"

"It would appear so. Honestly, I'm surprised that Foster's been able to keep him away this long."

"I'm not sure if I told you that Simon called Neil after we were reunited with Joe."

"No, I don't recall you telling me."

"There was so much going on in the first few days and weeks. We heard from hundreds of people. Simon reached out to Neil. They had a long chat. Neil said that he was quite gracious, happy that we had found him. Neil said that it was good to talk to Simon, but he felt like he was talking to someone that he hadn't been in contact with for decades. It has only been two or three years since we'd last seen Simon."

"Neil and Simon were never exactly close. They have very different personalities."

"True. Neil said that it was almost like talking to someone he didn't know at all. It made him wonder if the Simon we had gotten to know was not the one you lived with." Renee took the first bite of her banana split. "Oh, this is heavenly."

"What do you mean?"

"Simon was always nice to us, but we never thought it was real. Like he tolerated us to keep the peace."

"Renee, there was a time that I would have been quick to defend Simon and deny what you just said."

"Yes, I remember those days clearly."

"I'm not going to do that now. It took me a while to realize that I didn't really know Simon the way I thought I did or should have. I was genuinely shocked that he had an affair and left me. I wasn't necessarily surprised that we were divorcing. I did not expect our marriage to end in such a cruel way. Quite frankly, I might not recognize Simon if I spent any time with him now either. This man who is now abandoning his new family surprises me, too. His actions are speaking much louder than his words ever did."

"Did you have a good lunch?"

After a conference call later in the afternoon, Jenn emerged from her office to find that Doris had returned from lunch.

"I did. Hope your visit with Renee was good."

"It was. We celebrated our time together by eating banana splits at Quincy's. We felt like kids again."

Jenn watched Doris' expression. A look of nervous surprise crossed her face. Both women remained silent, staring each other down. Doris was the first to speak.

"I haven't had a banana split in years. With all that fruit, it should be considered health food."

The ding of the bell on the front door gave Doris a reprieve from Jenn's attention. Smiling at the person who entered, Jenn moved out of the way, heading toward the newsroom.

It was a mystery man.

"Hello, Jenn, how are you doing today?"

Helen Berry, the senior reporter for the newspaper, sat at the desk just beyond the Editor's office. A quick glance revealed that Lyle Livingston was not in his office.

"I'm doing great, Helen. Am I correct that you've been on an extended vacation?"

"Yes, my husband and I went on a road trip to the Grand Canyon. It was a bucket list trip for us. We decided earlier this year that we were going to start tackling that list before we retired. None of us have guarantees on how long we have in this life. We need to carpe diem, as the saying goes. I appreciate you allowing me to take two weeks off."

"I absolutely agree! You've worked hard. You deserve having a new adventure whenever it fits into your life. How's everything going in here this week?"

"Busy as usual. Shaun is at the high school interviewing some of the coaches. Tyler is at a school board meeting. I believe there is a public hearing about the future possibility of building a new middle school."

"Where's Lyle?"

"I believe that Lyle is at the Town Manager's office discussing annexation."

"That's still a hot topic. What have you been working on this week, Helen?"

"I've been doing interviews for the stories that will be featured in the next special section. I've also been assigned to work on a more in-depth story about your sister's family and that miraculous reunion."

"Oh." Jenn didn't recall Lyle mentioning that story to her.

"I believe that Lyle plans to talk to you about that first. We've had several readers email the newsroom asking for one. The citizens of Serendipity believe it is a local story since so many of those involved are either living here or used to be."

"That's true. Honestly, I told Lyle not to give it any more space than any other story. I didn't want our readers to think that it would get preferential exposure because I own the newspaper."

"I think that's just it, Jenn. There is no other story like it, at least not in recent memory. It's a special story with a happy ending which, face it, that's a rarity."

"I guess you're right. Let me know when you want to begin interviewing. I can make the introductions for you. We could even do them at my home. There's still quite a bit of investigating that's going on behind the scenes. I think that most thought that once Jonah was found, that would be the end of it. We were wrong. It was only the beginning."

"Justice must have its day. In this case, I would imagine that your family is especially interested in justice being served."

"My sister and her husband are. But they will never have true justice because no one can give them back those twenty years without their son. They are looking forward to the years ahead. But he was taken as a little boy and returned a man. There will never be justice for that. Additionally, the person who took him is long dead. His wife certainly played a role and will have to pay for that. She also did what appears to be a good job of keeping him alive and healthy. They feel many conflicting emotions. I think that Renee and Neil also feel some gratitude toward her. So many abducted children don't live twenty days, so twenty years is astounding."

"All of what you are saying will make a great interview. It's the heart of the story. This is what our readers want to know."

"We can certainly share that with them. Neil and Renee have been amazed by the outpouring of well wishes that have come from people from all over the world. They are being selective regarding the interview requests they accept. The list has been long. I'm sure they would not mind speaking with us though. I can use my clout to make that happen." Jenn laughed, winking. "Good to chat with you, Helen. I'm going to get back to the dozen or so emails that I'm sure have arrived in my inbox while I've been chatting to you."

"Thank you, Jenn. I'm enjoying working for you."

"I'm glad. I'm going to work hard to keep you feeling that way. Let me know if I don't toe the mark."

Passing through the lobby, she found Doris helping a visitor. Jenn returned to her office, surprised to find that Mel was stretched out on the couch.

"Hello, there. Did you need a nap, Ms. Snow?"

"I needed a hiding place." Mel did not move, except opening one eye.

"Who are you hiding from?" Jenn sat down at her desk.

"The loudest group tour I think we've ever hosted. It's a full motor-coach from a retirement village in Long Island, New York. The diversity in this group is quite interesting. There are people originally from fifteen different countries. But they were all in our little visitor center speaking each of their native languages. Imogene is handling it like a champion. My head is about to explode. I've been lying on your couch for ten minutes, and I can still hear their voices chattering in my head."

"You have the best stories, Mel." Jenn chuckled, while going through the latest email messages in her inbox. "I've got an email from your favorite car dealer."

"What does my honey bunny have to say?" Mel sat up, still holding her head.

"It's happy news for the *Serendipity Sun*. One of the vehicle brands he represents is launching a large new advertising campaign and will reimburse the dealership over half the costs of ads they run. Sinclair wants to do an additional full page ad once a week for the next three months. Wow! That's a chunk of change on top of the current contract. Ellie will be doing a happy dance."

"Bravo! That's fabulous."

"Are you still planning to go with him to that car dealer convention in a few weeks?"

"I think so. I've not officially confirmed yet because that may conflict with the small window of time that Mom and Dad will be home between trips. They've been gone so much over the last few months, I don't want to be gone while they are home."

"Where are they now?"

"Europe. They've been on a monthlong tour that touches almost every European country. It's their third visit to Europe, but the first time they are covering so much geography."

"Where's the next trip taking them?"

"Australia and New Zealand."

"A trip to the land down under."

"You know, I've heard Australia called that my whole life. I finally Googled it the other day to find out why that term is used. The answer simply is because of its location in the Southern Hemisphere. I thought there would be a more interesting story than that."

"Now, I'm going to have that song in my head the rest of the day. 'I come from the land down under.'" Jenn sang, slightly off-key.

"Ear worm courtesy of the Serendipity Visitors Bureau." Mel rose from the couch. "Thank you for my quiet time. I think the group should be happily headed to their hotel by now. I think I'll walk down to Quincy's and get Imogene a treat as a reward for her patience. Then, I've got to head to my folks' house to do a couple of things."

"Boss penance for making the staff handle the hard stuff."

"I like to think of it as rewarding hard work with something from a local business."

"Quincy's is always good for that. Renee and I had banana splits for lunch."

"That's one way to reward yourself. What have you two done to deserve that?" Mel walked toward the doorway.

"I think at this point the best answer would be that we survived."

"I'll accept that. Talk to me later, bestie." Mel waved, closing the door behind her.

With Mel gone, Jenn continued to review her messages. Looking at her calendar, she realized that she had a rare afternoon that didn't include a meeting of some sort. Her thoughts drifted to the wonderful man in her life, who had made such a difference to her and others. Was there any chance that he might also have a little non-scheduled time this afternoon and evening? Returning to her calendar, Jenn looked at the following couple of days. While appointments and tasks filled the time, there was nothing in view that would require much preparation work on her part. This afternoon might be the clearest break she had or would have for quite some time. Acting on the impulse, Jenn picked up her phone, quickly punching the button next to Randy's name to dial the call. He answered on the second ring.

"To what do I owe this pleasure, Ms. Halston?"

The sound of Randy's deep voice sent shivers down Jenn's spine. Simultaneously, it gave her a feeling of comfort unlike any she'd ever known.

"I see a rare gap in my schedule that begs to play hooky. I'm seeking an accomplice in my uncharacteristic behavior. I'm hoping that the stars have aligned for that person to be you."

"Do you have me under surveillance?" Randy's tone turned serious.

"No. Why? What's wrong?" Randy's answer confused Jenn.

"Nothing is wrong. I literally pulled into my driveway about ten minutes ago. I've changed clothes and am brewing a pot of coffee, wishing that my favorite girl was here."

"Perfect! What shall we do with this rare afternoon?"

"The ocean is a little choppy for an afternoon out on my boat. Would you like to take a drive somewhere?"

"You are always having to go somewhere. If you have a few hours to relax, I want you to be able to do that completely. Renee just got back from a quick trip to Raleigh; we had lunch earlier. She told me that she and Neil are going to take a spur-of-the-moment little getaway about an hour south. That means that for like two seconds, I have my house to myself. Why don't you meet me there? I'll quickly come up with something delicious to cook this afternoon. We can walk on the beach and snuggle on the couch watching movies."

"Something easy for you to cook. I don't want you spending all afternoon chopping vegetables and mixing ingredients."

"I'll stop at the grocery store and find the ingredients for a wonderful stew that can slowly cook this afternoon. You can help me chop the veggies. I'll get some snacks out of the deli for us to nibble on while we watch a movie."

"Sounds perfect. When do you want me to come over?"

"Whenever you can. You've got a key. I'm going to leave the office now and make one quick stop at the store. If you arrive before I do, please take Jasper for a walk."

"I can do that. Do you want me to bring anything?"

"Just your handsome self. I'm so happy that we get to spend a few extra hours together."

"Me, too. See you soon."

Chapter Six

Randy

Smiling from ear to ear, Randy set his phone down on the counter. Since he'd already brewed the coffee, he decided to put most of it into a large thermos. He and Jenn might want a cup after a windy walk on the beach. There was no sense in it going to waste. The remaining coffee would go into an insulated cup that he could drink on his way to her house.

An afternoon with Jenn would be like heaven. Ever since she returned to Serendipity, there never seemed to be enough time in either of their schedules to spend spontaneous time together like they would this afternoon. Since he was Serendipity's Chief of Police and Jenn was the owner of the local newspaper, their complicated and time-consuming careers kept them both hopping. Combine that with the unusual events of the return of Renee's and Neil's son and finding out that an international thief was posing as Jenn's rich neighbor left little time for relaxation and fun.

This was going to be a rare opportunity. He would do his best to make the time count. Randy sent a quick group text to his second in command

and lead sergeants telling them that he was planning to take the after-noon and evening off. Since Joe Davenport returned to their team, and Randy had hired two additional patrol officers and an investigator, his staffing level was in much better shape. It was a weekday afternoon; his team could handle whatever came their way.

The route he took to Jenn's house went right by a new business that had recently opened. Enchanted Flowers was a new floral shop that was owned by the daughter of a former classmate of his and Jenn's. Randy saw an advertisement in a recent edition of the *Serendipity Sun* and had made a mental note to stop one day and give them some business. Today was a perfect day.

Ten minutes later after a brief chat while the young woman put together a gorgeous collection of flowers in a Mason jar with several small multi-colored ribbons tied around it, Randy was back on the road. Glancing over at the beautiful bouquet that he'd secured in the seat next to him, Randy felt proud of himself. *Jenn will love these flowers.*

He decided that he would avoid the downtown district and take the 'scenic route' instead. Not many people would recognize him in his old pickup truck with a ballcap on his head. Randy normally didn't mind being recognized by citizens. He'd made a point to be an approachable police officer ever since he returned to his hometown. But this afternoon was special, he didn't want to be distracted, so he drove through a neigh-borhood that took him a little out of his way. He soon realized that he would be going past the home of Mel's parents. Randy's mouth watered thinking about the delicious homemade rolls and baked ham that Mrs. Snow would soon prepare for his department. No matter how far away she and Mr. Snow travelled on their retirement excursions, they were always home for Christmas and their annual delivery of goodies to the police department.

Slowing down, Randy noticed that someone was standing on the lawn near the Snow's driveway. Randy slammed on his brakes when he heard the sirens of an ambulance whip around him and pull into that same driveway. He immediately parked his vehicle, jumping out. Hurriedly walking toward the house, Randy realized that it was Mel who was frantically motioning for the ambulance. On the ground was Sinclair Lewis, Randy's close friend and the love of Mel Snow's life.

"Jenn, where are you right now?"

"I'm at home. I thought you would be here by now. Please don't tell me you were called into work."

Randy could hear disappointment in Jenn's voice. In a few seconds that tone would change to concern.

"I'm not at work exactly, but I've got some serious news. Before you get scared, I'm fine. Nothing has happened to me, but I am at the hospital."

"Oh, Randy! What's wrong? You are scaring me."

"Calm down. Let me tell you what happened." Randy took a deep breath. He was standing outside of the Emergency Room, the sirens of an ambulance approaching blared in the background. "I'm standing outside of the hospital right now, so you may hear some noises. I was on my way to your house, and I decided to take the back route through a few neighborhoods instead of going through downtown. I was driving down the street that the Snows live on, Mel's parents. As I was approaching their house, I saw someone standing outside and an ambulance passed me and pulled into their driveway."

"Mel's parents aren't supposed to be home. They are still on a trip to Europe, I believe."

"Yes, that's right. It was Mel who I saw standing in the yard. Jenn, Sinclair was there helping Mel do something. He started having chest pains. Mel had him sit down on the ground and she called 911. They have him in one of the exam rooms. Because Mel isn't his next of kin, the medical staff are reluctant to tell her anything. I'm about to play the police card and see what I can find out. I think it would be good if you came here. Mel is a mess."

"Absolutely! Are you at Mercy General?"

"Yes. Please be careful. It is not a critical situation at this point. Drive carefully."

"I will."

"Jenn?"

"Yes."

"I'm so sorry that we didn't get to have our afternoon."

"Randy, I'm thankful that you are there for Mel and Sinclair. That's more important than anything we were going to do. I'll be there as soon as I can."

When the called ended, Randy walked back through the sliding doors into the lobby of the Emergency Room. He found Mel sitting on the edge of her seat with her head in her hands.

"Hey. Have you heard anything else?"

Mel raised her head. Randy could see two vertical lines, one from each eye, where a stream of tears had fallen.

"They won't tell me anything. It's awful."

Randy sat down next to Mel, pulling her into a hug. He didn't normally use his police position to get special treatment, but this wasn't a normal situation. Randy knew that none of Sinclair's siblings still lived in Serendipity and Sinclair's children were at least an hour away. He would try to reach Sinclair's kids, but, in the meantime, Randy needed to know what to tell them.

"I called Jenn. She's on her way. You sit tight. I'm going to see what the medical staff will tell the Chief of Police."

"Thank you, Randy. I know you don't like to do that."

"He's my friend, too."

Randy walked over to the admission desk, showing his badge, he asked the clerk if she would let someone know that he would like to have an update on the status of Sinclair Lewis.

Continuing to stand at the entranceway into the exam rooms, a few minutes passed before a doctor came out. Randy was glad to see that it was Dr. Bowers. He'd met the doctor several times when they'd brought victims or criminals in for medical treatment.

"Chief, I didn't expect to see you here this afternoon."

"I didn't expect to be here, Doctor. I was on my way to a friend's house when I came upon Sinclair in distress at his girlfriend's parents' home. Sinclair doesn't have any family living in Serendipity anymore, but I'm going to try to reach his children. I think they are both near Seymour Johnson Air Force Base. I'd appreciate if you could share what I should tell them. I'd also like to ease the mind of that lady over there who was with him when he experienced his symptoms."

"Well, Chief, Mr. Lewis is still undergoing some tests. His condition is stable right now. We don't believe that he had a heart attack today, but we will be admitting him for observation. Some of the tests that we've already done indicate that he's had a minor heart attack in the past. From my conversation with him, he doesn't seem to be aware of that having occurred. That's even more of a reason for us to monitor him and get a cardiologist to evaluate his condition, so that we can get Mr. Lewis the treatment he needs going forward."

Dr. Bowers pointed to the admissions desk. The two of them walked to it.

"Dawn, this is Police Chief Randy Nave, will you please give him the names and phone numbers of the emergency contacts we found from the card in Mr. Lewis' wallet? The Chief will try to contact them."

"Yes, sir."

The clerk began typing on her keyboard. A couple of minutes later, she handed Randy a piece of paper with the contact information for Sinclair's son and daughter.

"Please tell me you found out something." Mel rose from her seat when Randy approached.

"Dr. Bowers says that Sinclair is stable. They do not believe he had a heart attack today."

"Oh, I'm so relieved." Mel put her hand to her heart. "I should never have asked him to come over and help me do some things at my folks' house. I should have hired a handyman instead. Are they going to release him?"

"No. Dr. Bowers is admitting him for observation. Even though he did not have a heart attack today, some of the tests have revealed that he had a minor one in the past. Sinclair does not seem to know anything about it. Dr. Bowers is going to have a cardiologist evaluate Sinclair and perhaps recommend a treatment regimen."

"Oh, that sounds serious."

"It may be. The good thing is that it was found and, hopefully, can be treated. Maybe this little incident was a good thing." Randy pulled Mel into a hug. "It certainly could have been a different outcome if Sinclair had been alone without any knowledge of having heart issues."

"I guess you are right."

From behind Mel, Randy could see Jenn walking through the sliding doors. Randy backed away so that Jenn could take over the hugging. Mel started crying again at the sight of her friend. Over Mel's shoulder, Jenn made eye contact with Randy.

"He's okay. They are going to admit him for observation. They discovered that sometime before today, he had a minor heart incident. Admissions has given me the contact information for Sinclair's children. I'm going outside and call them."

By the time Randy returned to the waiting room, Mel had calmed down. A multi-vehicle accident was filling up the emergency room. A couple of his team were surprised to see their Chief on the phone, standing on the sidewalk.

"Were you able to reach Sinclair's children?" Jenn patted the empty seat next to her, encouraging Randy to sit down.

"I was. They are both on their way. Hopefully, Sinclair will be in a room by the time they arrive."

"We've not seen Dr. Bowers anymore since you went outside." Mel took a long drink from a bottle of water that Randy had given her earlier. "Of course, it's been quite busy in here."

"Sinclair's daughter mentioned that she remembers him having a complete physical about a year or so ago. She said it wasn't too long before he bought the dealership. She doesn't know of any health issues other than some mildly high blood pressure."

"He takes a med for that. We told the EMT." Mel took a deep breath. "I'm so thankful that you were traveling by Randy. What were you doing in that neighborhood?"

"Randy was on his way to my house, Mel." Jenn made eye contact with Randy, giving him a brief smile. "We both had a little free time. I was going to make us some dinner."

"Oh, no. I'm so sorry. You two never have free time. We've messed up your afternoon. I will be fine now. You go back to your afternoon off."

"Absolutely not!" Jenn put her arm around Mel. "We are staying right here with you."

"Jenn's right. There's nothing more important than family and friends. You and Sinclair are really both in our eyes. I'm thankful that both of us were so readily available to be with you. It was meant to be." Randy stood up, seeing Dr. Bowers walking toward them.

"We are sending Mr. Lewis upstairs now. He's going to be on the fourth floor which is adjacent to the cardiac unit. You can follow him on the elevator down the hallway. Chief, were you able to reach Mr. Lewis' children?"

"I was and they are on their way."

"Great! Chin up, Mel. Mr. Lewis is going to be okay. Our head of cardiology will see him before the day is over and recommend a regimen of treatment." Dr. Bowers nodded in Mel's direction. "It's always a pleasure to see you, Chief. I've got to get back to our other patients."

After Dr. Bowers disappeared through the doors into the ER, Jenn turned to Mel.

"Dr. Bowers called you by your first name. Do you know him?"

"We've met. I wasn't sure if he would remember me. When he first moved here, I would say over fifteen years ago, we went out on a few dates." Mel smirked.

"Dating a doctor? Isn't a doctor supposed to be a good catch?" Randy chuckled.

"Not if your heart is set on a car dealer." Mel laughed.

"Let's go see Sinclair and give him a good talking to for scaring all of us." Jenn picked up her purse.

"I'll lead the way!" Mel briskly began walking toward the elevator.

"I'm sorry about our time together." Randy whispered while he and Jenn followed behind Mel.

"This scenario could have ended a lot differently. I'm thankful it didn't." Jenn bumped Randy with her shoulder. "I'm thankful for any time with you."

"The best thing about automatic slow cookers is that they turn themselves off."

Several hours later, after Sinclair was settled in his room and his children arrived, Jenn and Randy took Mel back to her parents' home to get her vehicle. It was time for dinner by then and that stew Jenn had begun cooking hours earlier.

"It smells heavenly." Randy accepted the bowl Jenn handed him. "I'm assuming it is a beef stew?"

"Yes, it's my twist on the famous Julia Child beef bourguignon. I adapted her recipe years ago to a slow cooker version. It was a great meal to have after my kids' sporting events, especially on a fall or winter evening."

"I'm glad that I see a full slow cooker of it. I'm starving."

"Take your time and enjoy it. I'm sure there will be enough for you to take home some leftovers as well. I'm going to sit here and enjoy my beautiful bouquet of flowers."

"I'm sorry that they had to hang out in my truck for several hours this afternoon, but it looks like they aren't any worse for it."

"Thankfully, it was a cooler day. They had ample water to keep them hydrated. I was so happy to learn that it was Meredith Sommers' daughter who opened this new shop."

"Yes, I saw the advertisement in the *Serendipity Sun*, and I told Julia how I learned about her shop. Julia moved here while Meredith returned to care for her father. After Mr. Sommers passed away, Meredith and Julia decided to stay."

"All roads lead back to Serendipity, it would seem." Jenn sat down across the table from Randy.

"Oh, Jenn, this is the most delicious stew I've ever eaten. Please promise me that you will make it frequently. I could eat this every week." Randy rolled his eyes while he took a second bite.

"Well, that's high praise." Jenn chuckled, handing Randy a bowl of sourdough rolls. "I was planning to put a peach cobbler in the oven this afternoon while we watched a movie, but, unfortunately, we were detained elsewhere."

"A cobbler would have been lovely, but I'm more than happy to make a meal off this stew and rolls. Our afternoon certainly didn't turn out like we expected, but I am glad that we were able to help our friends."

"Indeed. My spur-of-the-moment idea got sidetracked, but it was serendipitous that you happened to drive by the Snow home when you did. Mel appreciated you being with her."

"Honestly, I took that route to avoid driving through downtown. As the police chief, it's hard to drive or walk through the business district without someone stopping you. I was being a little selfish because I was anxious to spend time with you." Randy reached across the table, squeezing Jenn's hand, before taking a second roll.

"You can call it selfish, but it turned out that your helping nature knew that you were needed elsewhere. It all worked out for the best."

"I'll agree with that. If I hadn't stopped a few minutes to get those flowers, I might have missed the incident entirely."

"Everything happens for a reason. We still have a nice evening ahead of us." Jenn began to eat her serving of stew.

"I was glad that Sinclair's children were available to come immediately. Hopefully, they can be part of the conversations with the doctors to determine Sinclair's path of treatment. I'm sure that it was a surprise to him to learn that he'd already had a minor attack. I don't recall him mentioning anything about his health other than joking with me that we were getting old."

"I think we are about to reach the age when reality starts staring us in the face."

"Or kicking us in the tail." Randy took a long drink of water. "We are required to get annual checkups. This incident makes me want to go more often. I have no interest in becoming a statistic when I finally can spend my golden years with the girl of my dreams."

"Aww, that's mighty sweet, Chief Nave. I'm looking forward to the same thing. Maybe we should make doctors' appointments together."

"That's not a bad idea. Have you established yourself with a local physician yet?"

"I haven't. It's on a list that every week seems to get longer."

"Your health should be a priority, young lady. Especially when you could potentially be taking care of an old police officer one day."

"Yes, sir." Jenn gave Randy a little salute. "In the meantime, would the Chief like another serving of stew? I can see the bottom of your bowl."

"Yes, ma'am. My mother always said that it was rude to not accept a second helping. I wouldn't want to be rude. I may accept a third or fourth." Randy handed Jenn his bowl.

"I told you that you could take some of this home. You don't have to eat the entire pot in one sitting."

"Okay. Mom also said not to be a pig."

"No one within five miles of your mother's house ever went hungry. I remember her serving us rice pudding in coffee mugs on those rare snowy days we had in our childhood."

"Yep. Mom would not make rice pudding unless it snowed. It certainly made it a special treat."

The buzz of Jenn's phone drew her attention. She excused herself, stepping away to answer a call from her youngest daughter.

After Randy finished his second serving of stew, he began cleaning up the kitchen and washing dishes.

"You don't need to be doing that, Randy." Jenn took the last bite of her serving of stew before joining Randy at the kitchen sink.

"There's not much to do. You've had a long day, too."

"I'm going to put most of the leftover stew in glass pint jars. It will keep much longer than in plastic." Jenn began ladling the soup into the containers she'd chosen.

"It's not going to need to keep long at all. I'll be depositing it into this extra compartment within the next day or two." Randy rubbed his stomach. "I enjoyed this meal very much. I've not eaten any of your cooking that I didn't like, but this one is on my favorites list."

Jenn put the containers of stew into the refrigerator, then took the large bowl from the slow cooker to the sink. Bumping Randy away, she began washing it herself.

"There's a lot of tension in there, young lady." Randy began to rub Jenn's neck and shoulders.

"I wouldn't know why. I live such a stress-free life." Jenn rinsed the large bowl, laying it on the draining rack. "One of Emily's pieces of news is that she's considering going to law school."

"Is that a new interest?"

"Personality wise, not really. Emily always loved watching TV shows that featured prosecuting attorneys. I remember that sometime during her early elementary years, she pleaded her case to have her allowance raised. She even wrote a closing argument that she delivered during dessert one night. Her father and I weren't sure whether to be proud or afraid."

"She sounds like a young woman who knows what she wants. Am I correct that she's in graduate school?"

"Yes. She's about to finish her master's in business administration. We've always expected that she would head to Wall Street." Jenn finished cleaning the sink, then wiped her hands on the dish towel hanging nearby.

"I'm sure there are plenty of jobs for lawyers on Wall Street."

"No doubt. That's not what I would have imagined her doing. But life has a way of changing perspectives."

"Would sending her to law school be financially challenging for you and her father?"

Jenn poured two mugs of coffee, still warm in Randy's thermos, which he then picked up and carried into the living room.

"Surprisingly, it would not. Both my parents and Simon's started college funds for the kids when they were born. Amazingly, that money has never run out. The last I checked there was still enough in one of the funds for another child to go to college. Simon and I decided years ago that anything left in those funds would be the seed money to start funds for any grandchildren we might have. Emily can afford to go to law school. I can't help but wonder if this is a real career goal or a passing fancy because of something that has caught her interest."

Jenn picked up the television remote before she sat down on the couch next to Randy.

"Or someone?"

"What do you mean?" Jenn gave him a questioning look.

"Sometimes career choices can be influenced by another person, a professor or friend. Or maybe she's interested in someone who has decided to go to law school."

"Oh, I hadn't thought of that. Emily rarely ever mentions dating anyone. I certainly hope that I haven't been so caught up in my own life and the things that have been happening here that I've missed something important going on with Emily." Jenn frowned.

"Stop those worry lines, Momma." Randy ran his finger over Jenn's forehead. The action made her laugh. "You are a wonderful mother."

"I've also been a distracted one with everything going on with Renee and Neil, Foster and Michelle moving here, and Claire's world travels."

"You also have a new business to run and a tired old police chief following you around, but I think you still do an admirable job of being there for your kids. If anything, you give yourself to others too much and don't take care of yourself."

"That would be the pot calling the kettle black, don't you think?"

Jenn elbowed Randy a little, giving him the opportunity to pull her closer to him in an embrace.

"Guilty! I think that may be one of the reasons that we are getting along so well. Both of us are interested in the well-being of others. I think it's part of our DNA."

"I can't argue with that." Jenn snuggled closer. "Today is a good example. You were blessed to be at the right spot at the right time to help our friends. We still got to spend more time together today, just not the way we planned."

"Exactly. I think Sinclair may have dodged a bullet today. Most significant heart attacks are preceded by smaller, warning ones." Randy took a deep breath, thinking about his friend.

"It would be horrible if after all these years apart that Mel's and Sinclair's time together was cut short before it started. It makes you think."

"It certainly does." Randy thought about the woman sitting beside him. He stood on the sidelines all his life thinking that she was out of his reach. Now, in that moment, she was literally in his grasp. "You know, Jenn, I've been thinking about—"

A knock on the door interrupted Randy's chain of thought. Jenn jumped up to see who it was.

"I can't imagine who this might be. I've talked to everyone in my world today."

Randy waited on the couch. He couldn't let an interruption keep him from saying what was in his heart. *Life is too short to let a second chance pass you by.* Hopefully, whoever was at the door would be a quick visitor. They didn't need another problem disrupting what remained of their evening.

"Simon! What are you doing here?"

Randy rolled his eyes when his tired brain realized who that name belonged to. It was time for Randy to come face-to-face with the man who'd foolishly underestimated the value of a woman like Jenn. In a way, Randy had looked forward to this day. He had hoped that it was at a later stage of his life with Jenn, at the wedding of one of the children or the birth of a grandchild. A time when Jenn had a ring on her finger that matched one on his and she would introduce him as her husband.

Unfortunately, that day came sooner than expected and, in a location, where the awkwardness of the situation would be felt by all.

CHAPTER SEVEN

Jenn

"Hey, Babe, I decided it was high time I visited my family at the beach."

Simon pushed past Jenn walking from the deck into the kitchen like he did so every day.

"Simon, don't call me 'Babe.' If you are here to see *your* family, then your GPS should have taken you to Foster's address."

"Oh, you know that I always loved your parents' house. Who stays in a condo a couple of blocks from the beach when they can stay at a beach house with a view of the ocean?"

"Simon, I don't want to tell you that you are not welcome in my home. That's not who I am as a person." Jenn could feel Randy's presence behind her, just out of Simon's view. "But I'm not running a bed and breakfast either. If you are going to visit Foster and Michelle, you should be staying with them. Your automatic access to this house ended when we divorced."

"You are so caught up in this divorce thing. I'm still not sure it was the right resolution to our problems." Simon held up his hand before Jenn could speak. "I know that I am the one at fault in that scenario. I let a little middle-age crazy take hold of me. But I'm putting that mistake in my past. We were meant to spend our whole lives together."

Jenn could almost imagine the look on Randy's face. She secretly wished that he'd been working that evening and was still in his uniform. Before she could finish imagining that thought, she felt Randy's arm encircle her waist.

"Honey, is something wrong? I thought I heard voices."

Jenn was thankful that Randy chose another name of endearment to use instead of the one Simon did. *Randy can call me anything he wants.*

The shocked look that crossed Simon's face was followed by one Jenn was too familiar with—Simon looked annoyed. It was an expression that was more common than not with the man. When something didn't go his way, Simon usually didn't show anger as his first emotion. For that, Jenn had been thankful. Simon's look of annoyance was the equivalent of a toddler moments before throwing a tantrum. How could someone or something have the nerve to not go *his way*? To keep the peace, Jenn had caved to that behavior more times than she wanted to admit. Those days were over.

"Randy, this is Simon Young. He is the father of Claire, Foster, and Emily."

"Simon, those are some fine children you have there." Randy extended his hand. "Randy Nave."

"You know my children?" Simon looked at Randy's hand for a moment before he slowly shook it.

"I've met Foster in person, and only spoken to Claire and Emily several times when Jenn's been having FaceTime chats with them."

"I've heard about you. You are a police officer or something. You helped with the investigation that found Jonah."

"Randy is the Chief of Police. He led the investigation that found Jonah after all these years."

"Well, I will certainly shake your hand on that one."

This time, it was Randy who stared at Simon's hand for a moment, before shaking it again.

"Our family is quite grateful for the work that you and others did to find Jonah. Neil and I were discussing that the other day. It's amazing that someone can be found after being missing for twenty years."

Jenn closed her eyes, counting to ten. Simon was dropping Neil's name like they were blood brothers. At best, they'd tolerated each other because their wives were sisters.

"You and Jenn were neighbors growing up, right? Kind of like siblings, huh?"

Oh, boy.

"I had the biggest crush on Randy while we were growing up. I never imagined that I could have someone as wonderful as him in my life."

Even as the words were coming out of Jenn's mouth, she wasn't sure who was saying them. A quick glance in Randy's direction revealed what she'd already imagined, he was enjoying it.

'Annoyed Simon' was back.

"Uh, huh, well, I guess I should give Foster a call then, since it doesn't appear that I'm going to be staying here tonight." Simon reached for a cell phone that wasn't in his hip holster. "I must have left my phone in the car."

"Let me call him for you."

In one smooth move, like a police officer reaching for his gun in a movie, Randy's phone was off his hip with the numbers dialed.

"Hey, Foster, how are you doing this evening? I've been hearing all about that great remodel work that you and Joe are doing."

Jenn watched in amazement. She tried to control her composure. Inside, she was jumping up and down, giving Randy a 'high-five.'

"Sounds good. Listen, man, I'm here at your mom's house. She made me the most delicious beef stew. I think it's her much-improved rendition of one of Julia Child's recipes." Randy paused, listening. "Yes! That's the one! Anyway, we'd just finished dinner and were snuggling on the couch watching a movie. You will never guess who showed up at the door a few minutes ago?"

Jenn was going to bite her bottom lip off trying to keep from laughing if this conversation wasn't over soon.

"Oh, just give me the phone!" 'Annoyed Simon' couldn't take it any longer.

"I'll let you talk to the person. Give my best to Michelle." Randy grinned from ear-to-ear as he handed his phone to Simon.

"Foster, this is your father. I've come to visit. Have you got a place for me to stay, or do I need to find a hotel?" Simon stared daggers through Randy while he listened to his son. "Okay. Text the address to my cell phone. See you in a few."

Simon handed the phone back to Randy, and then turned his attention to Jenn.

"This is not how I imagined this evening was going to end." Simon began walking to the door.

"Me either, Simon. Foster's place is about a ten-minute drive. You shouldn't have any trouble finding it. The condo building is not too far from where the Alexanders used to rent a house every summer."

"The Alexanders? What in the world made you think of them?" Simon turned around giving her a scowl.

"Well, John Alexander was your best friend from college. We spent a lot of summers with them when the kids were small. I thought where they stayed might be a significant enough landmark to you."

"Whatever. I'll see you later. We've got some things to discuss." Simon walked out the door.

"You need to notify me in advance if you want to talk. My schedule is rather full these days."

Simon didn't respond. Only threw up his hand in a wave goodbye when he turned to walk down the steps to the driveway.

"That was interesting." Randy came up behind Jenn where she was still standing in the doorway.

Jenn did not say a word. She let her heart be her guide. Turning around to face Randy, she immediately put her hands on each side of his face, pulling him in to a strong kiss. Channeling all the aggravation she felt toward Simon into a passionate kiss for Randy—her hero, the man she knew was truly the love of her life.

"As far as I'm concerned, Simon can stop by any time he wants."

With Jenn standing on the deck and Randy inside the door, he pulled her closer. This time, it was Randy initiating the kiss.

I finally know what it feels like to be cherished by the man I love.

"Jenn! What a treat to have you visit me!"

Aunt Rachel greeted her niece at the front door. Jenn had scheduled to take lunch to an advertising client who had an emergency and cancelled mid-morning. She decided to take that time and food and share it with her aunt for a long-overdue visit.

"Thank you for allowing me to make a last-minute lunch date with you." Jenn carried in a large bag of food from her favorite catering business, More Please.

"Most of the time, last minute is not a problem for me. My social calendar is far from booked these days." Aunt Rachel led the way into her home after closing the door. "I thought we could have our lunch in the sunroom. It's lovely this time of day."

Jenn retrieved some plates and silverware as well as glasses for a pitcher of iced tea from the kitchen. By the time she'd returned to the sunroom, Aunt Rachel had taken the containers of food out of the bag, arranging them on the wicker and glass coffee table that sat in front of a loveseat and two chairs.

"This looks so delicious. I believe that I've enjoyed this company's food at some of my ladies' club luncheons in the past. As I recall, their name is an adequate representation of how you feel about eating their food."

"Indeed. Today, their entrée is a Thanksgiving sandwich with sweet potato fries."

"Oh, my goodness!" Aunt Rachel opened the sandwich after sliding it from the container onto her plate. "It's like an entire Thanksgiving meal in sandwich form. There's turkey, stuffing, mashed potatoes, gravy, and cranberry sauce between slices of bread. I believe this might be a knife and fork sandwich."

"I anticipated that. I've had this once before. It's heavenly. I hope it doesn't put us to sleep." Jenn poured each of them a glass of tea.

"I will have to tell an interesting story so that you don't get sleepy."

Jenn raised her eyebrows, wondering if her aunt might continue the conversation they had days earlier when she hinted of a secret from long ago.

"I'm always ready to hear your stories. I missed a lot of opportunities to learn more about you and our family all those years that I lived in Atlanta."

"We missed you, my dear. Paisley and I often spoke of you being too far away. It's the reason that she and your father left you the beach house. Even though they realized they would be gone, they wanted you to come home."

"I regret that I never managed to get home as often as I would have liked. We think we are too busy. I'm still making those mistakes. Maybe now, at least, I will make less of them because I am aware."

"When you get to the end of your life, you will not regret spending less time being busy. You will regret not spending more time with those who matter the most. Our souls yearn to connect with our soul family. We can be fortunate to have some of our soul family as our biological family. It doesn't have to be that way though. You can spend your whole life missing someone you barely knew."

From Aunt Rachel's expression, she looked like she was a thousand miles away, or, perhaps, a lifetime.

"Please, tell me about that person, Aunt Rachel. Tell me one of your secrets."

Jenn watched a smile slowly cross her aunt's face. She tilted her head to one side, then looked away for a moment. When her eyes met Jenn's, they were filled with tears.

"When I was still a teenager, I fell in love with a young man who worked for my father. His name was Richard Bergman. He was only four years older than me. It seemed like a lot more when I was fifteen and he was nineteen. It was a different time. It was not usual for girls who were still in high school to become engaged and even married. My parents were a little different. They wanted Paisley and I to go to college. They allowed us to date. My father was crystal clear with our suitors—his daughters were not getting married before they got an education. Period."

"They were smart parents, ahead of their time."

"They were. Despite this forward thinking, they were also quite traditional in other respects. Like all parents, they made mistakes."

"You and Mother both completed degrees. You used yours. Mom never did."

"Paisley did not. She fell into the traditional role of wife and mother quite naturally. My father kept Carson so busy with the business, it would have been difficult for her to juggle raising her three girls and hold down a secular job."

"We always saw you as career-oriented since you weren't married." Jenn hoped the question would open a window for further discussion about Aunt Rachel's life.

"You're getting ahead of yourself, young lady. Do you want to hear a secret or not?"

"Yes, ma'am. I'll eat my lunch being quiet." Jenn took her knife and fork, cutting into the sandwich and taking her first bite. "Yum."

"It is delicious. I will eat slowly while I talk." Aunt Rachel took another small bite. "As I was saying, I dated a young man named Richard. He came from a nice local family. The Bergmans had strong roots in the area. You would not find anyone by that name here now, but some distant relatives remain. Richard fell head over heels in love and quickly became quite devoted and serious about me. Looking back, I would say that I was infatuated with him. At the age of fifteen, I was not old enough to truly be in love, but I did feel love for him. He worked in Father's construction business for about a year after high school, then decided that he wanted to enlist in the Army and try to make that a career. He pleaded with my father to allow me to marry him when he came back from completing boot camp. Carson Frederick would have none of it. He liked Richard well enough for him to have been a son-in-law one day, but he was firm in his resolve that his two daughters were completing their educations."

"Marrying at fifteen or sixteen sounds like a punishment. I'm certainly glad we moved away from that being a norm, at least in this country." Jenn swirled a sweet potato fry in the homemade ketchup that came with the order. "Goodness, don't forget to try the ketchup. It's quite unusual, sweet and tangy."

"At the time, I do not think that most young women saw it as a punishment. 'Playing house' was probably the most popular game that girls were taught to play. It certainly seems limiting when compared to today's opportunities. Honestly, even without my father's strict mandate, I don't think I would have been interested in marrying that young. I did have several friends who married during their junior year in high school. One had a child during our senior year. She lived a long and happy life. I attended her funeral about a year ago. She had over one hundred descendants."

"Wow! That's mind-boggling."

"When you start young and have a big family, each generation is larger." Aunt Rachel ate a fry with ketchup as Jenn suggested. "The fries are good. I'm not a fan of the ketchup though. I think I'll stick with eating my sandwich and reheat those fries for dinner with my own ketchup." Aunt Rachel took one last bite before closing the lid on the container of fries.

Jenn momentarily checked her phone. She didn't have another appointment until four o'clock but needed to make sure that she kept an eye on the time. Listening to her aunt tell stories would make the afternoon pass quickly.

"Richard was shipped overseas, and his first tour of duty was in Europe. Before he left, he gave me a promise ring and asked me to not date any other boys. I honored his request as best as a teenager who liked to go to dances could." Aunt Rachel winked. "He wrote to me every week. I still have every letter in an old suitcase upstairs in a closet."

"Can I read them sometime?"

"If you come to visit me more often." Aunt Rachel raised an eyebrow and nodded her head.

"Time passed. Richard's assignments took him to other parts of the world, and he rose in rank. Each time he came home on leave, he was more determined for us to marry. I graduated high school and entered college. He came home for Christmas during my sophomore year of college. During that visit, he asked my parents if he could propose. My father agreed with the understanding that the engagement would have to be until I had at least graduated. Richard presented me with a beautiful antique ring that had belonged to his grandmother. During that visit, we spent a lot of time talking about a future together. He still planned to make the Army his career. I began to see myself travelling around the world as his wife. While I had loved him from the start, it was during that visit that I began to be *in love* with him and in love with a life we might be able to create."

"Why is it that I didn't have any Uncle Richard then?" Jenn began to smell the beginnings of a not-so-happy ending. She was feeling a little disappointed.

"The reason is because a month after he went back on duty, his letters stopped."

"I guess I should have known this story was going to have some twists and turns."

"You're not prepared for how curvy this road is going to get. I suggest you eat up and put on your seatbelt. It's going to be a wild ride."

Jenn furrowed her brow while taking another bite of her sandwich. Maybe there was a good reason that her mother refused to tell Aunt Rachel's story.

"As I said, Richard left after his visit home. While I wouldn't say that he was completely secretive about his missions, he never offered many details in his letters. He was a courier. At that time, the job entailed him being given important documents, some top secret, that needed to be transported from one high-ranking officer to another. Email did not exist back then, of course, nor did fax machines. His work was not typically dangerous, but Richard was travelling from one part of the world to another and that involved a certain level of risk. Apparently, his assignment right after he returned to service from his visit home took him quite close to enemy lines. The only details I heard at the time was that the plane he was on was shot down. His parents were informed that he was missing in action, or MIA. In the years since, I've come to learn that can be a quite ambiguous and cruel term. It basically means that it is not known what happened or the military does not want to reveal what happened. It would be years before the Army officially declared him dead, even though there were no remains ever found. Richard's father was convinced that his son became a prisoner of war because the aircraft was found, but the only remains found were that of the pilot."

"Oh, Aunt Rachel, I'm so sorry. How heartbreaking that must have been for you at such a young age."

"That story did not have a happy ending. The reality is that the story of Richard and I didn't have an ending at all. Whether he died the day the plane went down or sometime thereafter, he would certainly be gone by now. I can't help but wonder though what his final days were like. I know I was on his mind and in his heart. He has certainly been on mine." Aunt Rachel set her partially eaten plate of food on the table in front of her. "Will you put these leftovers away, my dear? While you do that, I will find a photograph of Richard to show you."

Jenn did as Aunt Rachel instructed, gathering up the remains of her aunt's lunch and putting the leftovers away. She also cleaned up the trash from her own lunch, washing their plates and utensils. When she was finished, Aunt Rachel's immaculate kitchen was back to order. Looking around that room reminded Jenn of her own mother's tidiness and that of her Grammie Elana. There was a place for everything, and everything had a place.

When Jenn returned to the sunroom, she found Aunt Rachel with a large, old photograph album on her lap. Jenn stopped at the doorway, watching her beloved aunt. The woman was gently stroking a photo that took up a whole page in the album, whispering to it. While Jenn was too far away to see it, she could see that it was old, and sepia toned. Like the memory the woman was remembering, the photo was from another time.

"I see you standing there. Come on over here so you can see my Richard." Aunt Rachel looked up, beckoning Jenn with her eyes.

Jenn sat on the loveseat next to her aunt as the woman picked up the photo album and balanced it on her lap. Jenn had long thought that there was a magical quality to photographs as old as the ones before her now. After so many decades had passed, it was as if time was standing in suspension so that those who came after could have a glimpse into another world.

The large photo Jenn saw from across the room was one of those official photos that the military took of their solders. Jenn's thoughts went to Randy for a moment, thinking about that fateful day in their early twenties when he came to the newspaper while he was on leave. Like handsome young Richard, Randy had a world of dreams inside his heart of a future with someone. Jenn said a silent prayer of thanks that unlike her aunt, she now had the opportunity to live out some of those dreams with him.

"This is Richard. He was so young and handsome in this photo. I cannot imagine what he would have looked like if he'd had been allowed the gift of growing older. My heart holds him just as he looks here. How I wish he could jump off the page and speak to us now! His poor parents died of broken hearts not knowing whatever happened to him. It is another reason to be thankful that Jonah was returned to us. Many times, over the years, I have seen the same expression in Renee's and Neil's eyes that I saw with Richard's parents. Not knowing can be worse than the dreaded truth."

"Was it difficult to grieve for someone you weren't completely committed to? I imagine that through the span of time there have been countless young women who have mourned the loss of 'almost husbands.'"

"That's an interesting way to put it, Jenn. I do not think that I mourned Richard properly. While I did have devoted feelings toward him, I harbored a great deal of guilt that I didn't feel like I'd loved him enough. The truth of the matter is that for most of our relationship I was too young to completely grasp and form the deeper feelings that he had for me. While certainly young himself, Richard was a few years older and had experienced vastly more of life. He had enough maturity, forced maturity perhaps, to have a clearer understanding of what he wanted for his future and who he wanted to spend it with." Aunt Rachel ran her hand over the photograph again, releasing a deep sigh. "Oh, Jenn, that guilt fueled my impetuous nature and caused me to act out of character in the years shortly after."

The grandfather clock that had stoically stood in the hallway of the Frederick house for close to a century chimed three times. Not believing it could already be that time, Jenn looked at her watch.

"Oh, Aunt Rachel, I'm going to have to leave. I don't want to. I want to stay and hear your story. Please promise me that you will continue when I can arrange to return."

"This was enough time travel for one day." Aunt Rachel closed the album, placing it on the table in front of her. "There are certainly more tales to be told from this long life of mine. I hope to be blessed with more time to tell them."

The last comment weighed heavy on Jenn's heart while she hugged her aunt before leaving. The sudden passing of Jenn's mother gave her a stark lesson in the lack of guarantees in life. Jenn would make Aunt Rachel a priority, like the care and respect she gave business appointments on her schedule.

"After the meeting I am heading to, I will look at my calendar and text you some possible times when I could come back."

"My schedule is not that complicated, Jenn. You come back whenever you can."

Aunt Rachel followed Jenn to the front door. Once Jenn reached her Jeep, she noticed that her aunt continued to stand at the doorway, waving. Jenn thought about the story of Richard. Often a younger generation looked at an older one never imagining that they might have gone through similar happy or sad moments in their lives, problems and disappointments. Driving back to her office, Jenn wondered what secrets her own mother held in her heart that she never shared. Jenn began to realize that she might only know what was 'on the surface' of the past, even in the lives of those she'd been the closest to her entire life.

"I'm ready to hear a positive update about Sinclair. Has he been released from the hospital?"

On her way back to the office after her meeting, Jenn stopped in at the Visitors Bureau. Imogene let Jenn in before she left for the day.

"He was released this afternoon. His daughter came and took him home. Sinclair has agreed to let her stay overnight, just in case he needs something. His new regimen begins tomorrow."

"What does that mean?"

"It means that he needs to stop eating like he's a teenager."

Jenn could see exhaustion on Mel's face. Sinclair's health scare had taken a toll on her best friend.

"I'm exaggerating a little. The tests showed that probably sometime in the last year, Sinclair had a minor heart attack. There was only slight damage, but enough to provide a warning for the future. Sinclair's blood work wasn't off-the-charts or anything, but several of his results are borderline and heading to a problem area. He does need to get a little weight off and watch his diet. The hospital suggested that he sign up for the cardio health program at the wellness center. He said he was going to ask Randy if he'd do it with him, but I also think I may sign up. I could certainly lose a few pounds, too."

"Maybe the four of us should commit to this together."

"You're quite fit as it is, Jenn."

"I may be within my target weight, but it doesn't mean I'm really fit. Those planned walks and runs I was going to do on the beach got sidetracked by the imposter who lived next door."

"That reminds me. Have you heard anything further about the legalities of the transfer of the Bentley property?"

"We're swimming in a sea of attorneys and it's far from where we want to be. I'm intentionally not keeping up with it, and I believe Renee has adopted the same position. We will let the legal teams work it out, and we will deal with the next steps once the transfer is made."

"You and your sisters owning the Oasis. It's incredible."

"It's incredibly scary. I can't imagine how we are going to make this work." Jenn held up her hand before Mel could say anything else. "I came here to find out how Sinclair was doing and catch up with my bestie."

"I appreciate it. Things are better than they were. It scared me half to death, Jenn. After all these years, I have Sinclair back in my life. It terrified me that he could be gone so quickly." Mel began to cry. "I want to have a chance."

Jenn knew there was a world of feelings building up in Mel. It was the core of the reason why she stopped by. Mel had been fortunate not to suffer the loss of any close loved ones so far. She was in her mid-fifties and still had both of her parents. It was a reality that Mel had yet to deal with, but Jenn knew her friend would understand how close it could come.

"You've not lost your chance. I'd say that this probably scared Sinclair, too. He will work hard to make his heart healthy. It has fallen in love all over again with the girl of his dreams. This scare was another second chance. Take hold of it with both hands and use the knowledge wisely. If he doesn't behave himself, be relentless. We will all work together on our health so that the four of us can have many years ahead together."

Jenn pulled Mel into a firm embrace. The sobs subsided.

"You knew I needed you to come, didn't you?"

"I suspected that you were holding too much in, trying to be strong." Jenn held Mel at arms' length. "Brave is important in the heat of the moment. Those emotions need to eventually be released. It's healthy to let it out.

"That's right." Mel picked up her purse and laptop case. "With everything going on, you've not explained how the surprise visit from Simon went the other day."

"Well, surprise barely covers it, mortified is a better word. If he had to show up at my house though, Simon's timing couldn't have been better. As I believe I mentioned in my text, Randy and I had finished a late dinner after returning from the hospital. Randy and I haven't discussed it since, but I think he enjoyed it. He didn't miss a beat in his conversation with Simon, including calling Foster from his own phone and chatting like they were long-time friends."

"Oh, I bet that was a big hit with Simon." Mel rolled her eyes.

"Simon was ill-equipped to go up against Randy. I enjoyed the exchange immensely. Foster told me later that his father was quite perturbed by the time he arrived at their condo. He doesn't think that Simon will visit again for a while. I hope that he gives up his silly idea regarding buying a condo here."

"I hope I don't run into him when he does visit." Mel turned off lights throughout the office while they were walking out. "Anything else interesting going on? I'm almost afraid to ask that with the way life has gone recently."

"I had a spontaneous visit with Aunt Rachel this afternoon. I'm going to make sure that I spend more time with her. I am beginning to realize how little I know about her life. I think the same was true with my own mother. I'm going to encourage you, Mel, to have some long chats with your parents. Ask them about their lives before you. Ask all the questions that dig to the deep details you'd like to know. Even ones that you think may be too personal or you won't like the answers. I wish I'd done more of that with my own parents. My mother's sudden passing is a good example of why everyone should do that."

"If they would stay here long enough for me to have that opportunity."

Jenn led the way out of Mel's office toward the front door of the building.

"What do they have to say about Sinclair being back in your life?"

"We managed to squeeze a dinner in with them during one of the times they were home. Everyone was cordial. It was a little awkward, at first. That feeling quickly passed when Sinclair and Dad started talking about vehicles." Mel locked the door behind them. "Privately, they've said they want me to be happy. Everyone makes mistakes in life and what happened was a long time ago. They were quite upset to learn that Sinclair had a heart incident while he was doing some work at their house."

"I'm sure it was hard for them to see you hurt, but they also realize what happened when we were young cannot be undone. Forgiveness is a powerful gift, isn't it?"

Jenn crossed the street with Mel to a downtown parking lot. They both waved at Amelia Lowe, owner of Sew What, who was getting in her car a few vehicles away.

"I've got to shake this scared feeling and concentrate on Sinclair, and the rest of us, having a healthy future. I'm not going to blow this second chance. I'm anxious to spend some time with the Halston sisters. I've seen Amber a few times through the years, but not near enough to feel like I know her anymore."

"She should be back soon. We haven't gotten deep into the details yet, but Renee and I are planning to have a party for Aunt Rachel's eighty-fifth birthday. We are hoping to be able to have it at the Oasis."

"Oh, my goodness! That would be fabulous! You might as well plan for the invitation list to be long. Rachel Frederick is beloved in Serendipity. You could probably get sponsors to help you host it. I'm not kidding."

"Funny that you say that, because one idea Renee had was to somehow also make it a fundraiser for a local organization that is special to Aunt Rachel. We know that she will not want gifts. It would also be appropriate to make it a philanthropic event since it's being held at the Oasis."

"This idea is sounding better and better. Sign me up for the committee." Mel's eyes sparkled with excitement. "When is her birthday?"

"She will be eighty-five on December 31. From what I remember from hearing the story, she was born very near midnight."

"Jenn! A New Year's Eve party in honor of Rachel! At the Oasis! As a fundraiser! That is a recipe for a fabulous event. I think I'll go home and start planning what I'm going to wear."

Mel gave Jenn a strong hug before getting into her vehicle. She began to pull out of the parking lot as Jenn started walking down the street back to her office.

"I'm thankful for my bestie." Mel stopped to let Jenn walk in front of her vehicle, rolling down the window. "You've always known when my heart needed your words of encouragement and love. I don't know how people survive without a lifelong best friend."

"Me, either." Jenn smiled. "It would sure make for a big hole in my life."

CHAPTER EIGHT

Joe

JOE TOOK A LONG, slow breath to calm his nerves. Standing behind the prison guard, he waited for the burly man to press the button that would trigger the large mechanical door to open, allowing Joe his first experience deep inside a prison. Even though he'd clocked about a year of police duty during his initial time on the Serendipity Police Department, Joe never had a reason to be closer than the transport drop-off location of this, or any other, holding facility.

Honestly, he never would have imagined that he would visit anyone in prison, unless perhaps he delved into detective work later in his career. The fact that Joe was there to see the woman he'd known as his mother for twenty years was beyond any scenario he could have dreamed for his life.

The door opened. Joe followed the guard across the concrete floor, down a short hallway to another large door with another button controlling its movement. It must take some getting used to, even if you only worked there, to hear the door behind you close before the one in front of you would open. He'd lost count on how many doors had closed behind him already. Joe shook his head, a chill running down his spine with the thought. *How could you ever get used to this?*

He'd written down the name 'Samantha Fairfield' at the first main desk he'd encountered. Today was a visitors' day, but Joe's pending arrival had been announced a couple of days earlier by the District Attorney's Office to the Warden of the facility. This would not be the ultimate place where Samantha Fairfield would serve whatever time the judicial system deemed appropriate for her crime, but it was the place where she would be confined until her trial and the sentencing thereafter.

"Have you been here before?" The guard spoke for the first time to Joe.

"No, sir."

"You will go through this door. There is a chair for you to sit in. You will be separated from the inmate by a glass partition. There's a phone for you each to use to talk. I'll let you know when your time is up, or you can knock on the door if you are ready sooner."

Joe nodded as the officer opened the door.

"You know this Fairfield woman kidnapped a kid many years ago." The officer stood in the doorway for a moment.

"Yes, sir. I know. I was the kid."

A surprised expression crossed the guard's face before he closed the door behind him. A few minutes later, Joe had to look down for a moment when he caught the first glimpse of his mother as she came through the door on the other side of the glass. The difference in her appearance was shocking.

Sitting down in the chair on the other side of the partition, Samantha jumped slightly when the guard closed the door behind her. She stared at Joe, expressionless, for several minutes, not attempting to pick up the phone on her side of the glass.

Joe used those moments to study the woman, trying to conjure in his mind a memory of what she looked like before she began wearing the orange jumpsuit that glaringly contrasted with the paleness of her skin. If it was humanly possible, Joe believed that the few strands of gray that had been in her mousy brown hair had multiplied ten times in the couple of months she'd been incarcerated. Her normally thin frame could now be called frail. He could see the bones in her arms. The rosiness of her cheeks was replaced by the skin tone of someone who never saw the sun. A feeling of anger rose inside of him. *Woodrow did this.* His thoughts jumped to the two people he now knew as his parents and the twenty years they lived in their own prison. He focused on Samantha Fairfield again. *You could have ended this long ago. You might not be sitting here now.*

His visit today was about learning some answers. Randy had advised him that if there were things he wanted to know from Samantha, that he better ask questions before they got too deep into the trial. His access to her might be limited then. More than anything, Joe wanted to know *why*. Why was he taken? Why didn't Samantha try to get away from Woodrow and take him back? Why?

Joe pointed to the phone before picking it up. Samantha continued to stare straight ahead. He was beginning to wonder if she was mentally in there at all. Gently, he tapped on the glass. Samantha flinched. She finally made eye contact, before picking up the receiver on her side of the glass.

"Hello." Joe's voice was soft and gentle.

Samantha did not respond.

"I wanted to come and see how you were doing."

Silence continued.

"You've lost a lot of weight. Aren't you eating?"

Nothing.

Joe took a deep breath, running his hand through his hair. His mind raced with all the questions he planned to ask. Maybe one of them would prompt a response.

"I wanted to ask you some questions."

Samantha made eye contact with him.

"I want to know why Woodrow took me. Was this something that he did frequently? Did he kidnap children and sell them or something?"

The information from the investigation that had been shared with Joe thus far indicated that Woodrow had been a hitman of sorts and a courier for some level of mafia. While there was nothing that had come out of the investigation so far, that Joe knew about, to indicate that Woodrow was trafficking children or anything like that, Joe was still curious.

"You were the only child."

Joe waited for Samantha to reveal something else. She was silent.

"But he took other people? He killed other people?"

"Woodrow did bad things. He didn't tell me about them." Samantha's expression did not change.

"Why did he take me then?"

"Because I wanted a child." Samantha briefly made eye contact. "I didn't think he would take me seriously. He rarely did."

"He took me for you."

Joe had heard the theory before. Somehow hearing it come out of his own mouth gave it new meaning. This time when Samantha made brief eye contact, there were tears in her eyes.

"Why didn't you make it right? Why didn't you take me and run away? You could have taken me back to my family. It was all over the news." Joe felt the emotion growing inside him. He heard it in his voice.

"I wanted to keep you. God help me! I wanted to keep you. I was a mother without a child."

"You made another woman into a mother without a child for twenty years. You made a father that way, too. Grandparents, aunts and uncles, cousins. There was a big family waiting a few hours away for a little boy named Jonah who never came home."

"They will have you now."

"They should have had me all along. You deprived them of that."

"Woodrow took you."

"You kept me."

"I loved you every day."

"That doesn't make it right."

A silence hung between them. Joe's feelings were warring inside. Sitting before him was the woman who had been the only mother he could remember. He'd been devoted to her in every way a son could be. However, now he knew the truth. It was supposed to set you free. It only made his heartache worse. After having met all those who were his true family, it made him angry to think about what he had missed. Instead of the stolen love of this woman who sat before him, he could have grown up in the unconditional love from his real family.

He had one final question.

"If you could go back and undo it, would you?"

"I would not have given you up." There was a tremble in Samantha's voice, but her answer was firm.

"Then, it would appear your love was not unconditional. What you wanted came before what was right for me. I thank you for making sure that I was safe. All those years, you were the true force in my life. You were the person who allowed me to hold on in the train wreck of a life we lived with Woodrow. Now, I know that was all a lie, too. You were an accomplice in the crime against my life, my rights. I will not be coming back. Good luck, Samantha Fairfield."

Joe hung up the phone. He immediately got up from his chair and knocked on the door. Turning briefly back toward the partition, Joe saw Samantha bent over with her head in her hands. A twinge of sadness filled his heart for the woman. He knew her sadness was great. It was a glimpse of what Renee Davenport had gone through twenty years ago and every day since.

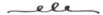

"I went to see Samantha Fairfield, like you suggested." The following day, Joe stopped by the Chief's office when the early shift he'd worked was over.

"I wondered if that might be what you were doing on your day off. How did that go? Did you ask the questions you wanted to?"

"Some of them. I guess I got the answers I expected. They were hard to hear though."

"Do you want to talk about it? Come on in and close the door behind you."

Joe crossed over the doorway, closing the door behind him. Sitting down in one of the armed chairs in front of the Chief's desk, Joe bowed his head thinking about the conversation.

"She admitted that Woodrow took me because she wanted a child."

"That's basically what Samantha said the day the Sheriff and I came to your house. From what I've heard from some of the investigators, Woodrow did a lot of dirty work for whatever mob or mafia he was working for." The Chief sipped his coffee.

"Yes, but he didn't take children. I was the only one, according to Samantha. I asked her why she didn't do the right thing and return me to my family. She said that she wanted to keep me. She was a childless mother. I asked her if she would do anything different, if she could go back. She said again that she would keep me. Samantha Fairfield doesn't have any remorse. Her being a mother was more important than where the child came from." Joe bit his bottom lip, holding back the emotion. "She always treated me well. She protected me from Woodrow as much as she could. Now I understand why I didn't receive any love from him. It was all a lie. She put her desire for a child ahead of the welfare of the child. The conversation was what I needed to be able to break ties. Love that is built on lies and deception is not love. I missed the life I could have had because of the one Samantha wanted. I'm done."

"I'm sure that is not an easy emotional place for you to be. But you are correct, your whole existence with her was based on a lie. Speaking as a parent, it's the exact opposite of what most of us strive to do. The other side of this equation is that even if you wanted to have some level of a relationship with her, it will be difficult. I do not see any judge or jury going easy on her. She will probably spend the rest of her life behind bars. This is a crime against a child and a crime against the sanctity of parenthood. I've dealt with a lot of serious criminals in my career. Most have a soft spot for children."

"I had to go see her. I needed to be certain about how I feel. Renee and Neil have not said anything to me about my future relationship with Samantha. They've not tried to influence me in any way. I respect that and appreciate it. I am starting to realize though what a horrendous ordeal the last twenty years have been for them. I don't want to disrespect them. I am grateful to Samantha Fairfield that she kept me alive. Looking back, I know that was not always an easy thing to do with Woodrow in the picture. I always felt like he wished I didn't exist. That makes sense now. As an adult and a police officer, I know there are a lot of children in this world who need a good home and loving care. You don't have to steal one."

"That's true."

Joe watched the Chief furrow his brow, deep in thought. Joe could tell that he was preparing to speak.

"I certainly do not in any way condone what Samantha did. It was wrong twenty years ago and it was wrong every day since. She had ample opportunities, even in the last few years to tell you the truth." Chief Nave took a deep breath. "We don't know her whole story though. We don't know what her mental state truly is. We will let the justice system decide her fate."

"That can't happen soon enough for me, Chief. I want to put this behind me. I don't want to be the 'child that was taken' for the rest of my life. I want to take my experience and do something good with it by helping others. I don't want to keep reliving it. I know that I've missed a lot of the life I could have had. From now on, I want to concentrate on the future and enjoying the people and experiences in it. I don't want to live in the past or focus on what I didn't have."

"That realization shows a maturity beyond your years, young man."

"Thank you. Finding out that the bulk of your life was a lie will do that to you." Joe stood up to leave.

"Remember, Joe, even though your identity was concealed from you, you still had real experiences that were important and meaningful. Like that carpentry teacher who took you under his wing. He made an important impact on your life. I'm sure if you think about it, there were many genuine people in your life, everywhere you lived. All those small impacts have made you into the man you are." Chief Nave stood up, reaching out to shake Joe's hand.

"You're right, Chief. Just like the man standing in front of me now. He's the epitome of genuine. I'll always be grateful that you came into my life." Joe returned the strong handshake he received, before leaving the room.

Focus on the good things, Joe. The future is good.

"Megan, this is delicious. Where did you learn to make Mexican lasagna?" Foster had a big bite on his fork, ready to consume.

It was potluck night at Foster's and Michelle's. Megan had accompanied Joe and brought the main dish.

"There's a restaurant downtown called La Siesta. We all need to go there sometime soon. You will love it." Megan served herself a portion of the dish. "It's a family-owned operation. I worked there for four years. I started out as a server but eventually became a cook and a supervisor. This is one of the dishes that we would sometimes do as a special. It's not on the regular menu."

"It's so fresh with a great mixture of ingredients." Michelle took a second bite. "I don't think I've ever had a version of lasagna that had chicken in it. Delicious."

Joe watched as Megan described how the dish was prepared in an animated conversation with Michelle and Foster. It was wonderful having these people in his life. Even though the four of them were only in the beginning of their friendship, there was already a comfortableness that often took years to develop. He couldn't help but smile between chews.

"Do you always smile while your chewing, Cuz?" Foster teased Joe. "Or are you trying to stay on your girlfriend's good side?"

"I certainly want to stay on Megan's good side." Joe winked in her direction. "The real reason I'm smiling though, besides this wonderful meal, is that I'm happy. I feel a happiness being around all of you, the extended Halston family, and my fellow officers at the PD. It's unlike any happiness that I've ever experienced before. Well, I guess that's not entirely true. I bet I was happy as a kid before my life changed. I don't have many clear memories of that time though."

Megan reached over, squeezing Joe's hand. When their eyes met, he saw so much love. Overcome with emotion, Joe's eyes pooled with tears.

"See what you've done, Foster." Joe wiped his eyes with his napkin. "I'm still smiling though."

"Okay, I'll quit. Let me tell you about my big sister who's about to hit town. She's not going to want me to remind you of this. I'm her little brother. It's my responsibility to wreak a little havoc on her life now and then. You had a nickname for Claire when we were little, running around the beach at our grandparents' house."

"I did? You've got an incredible memory, Foster."

"I'm not trying to make your eyes get wet again, but losing you was quite traumatic on Claire and me. We loved our cousin Jonah. He was our first pal. Our families got together every couple of months, even though we lived hundreds of miles apart. Our memories of you are strong."

Joe could feel the emotion rising again. He nodded.

"Anyway, the nickname you had for Claire was Bossy."

"Bossy? Why did he call her that?" Megan asked.

"Basically, because Claire was bossy. She was the oldest and she enjoyed telling us what to do. Jonah wasn't the least bit scared of her." Foster laughed, heartily. "I loved that part. I was the little brother who lived with her. She could love me with a vengeance or make my life miserable."

"Having a brother or sister would be great." Joe's thoughts came out before he could stop them.

"I'll be your brother, man. We were on the road to that when we were kids, we can do it again."

The emotions rippling through Joe were overwhelming. Quickly, he turned his attention back to the topic of Claire.

"Can I ask why Claire's marriage is ending? Do we not like the guy she's married to?"

"Derek is a great guy. I don't think there is anything that either of them has done to cause the dissolving of their marriage, except for marrying the wrong person. There's always been a lot of friendship and love between them, just not the kind that bonds a couple. We were all surprised they got married."

"They always seemed very comfortable together, but more in a close friend way than a romantic one." Michelle passed around more of the side dishes. "I don't think Claire has been happy for a while. A complete change will do her good."

"She will certainly be happy living here." Joe took a large bite of lasagna.

"Absolutely! Who wouldn't love living at the beach?" Foster served himself more salad. "Mom may be wishing for more privacy soon though. She's been back in Serendipity less than a year and almost the entire family has followed her."

"I think Aunt J loves having a lot of people around," Joe chuckled, "except international criminals living next door."

"That was one wild situation, for sure. I'm relieved that person was caught. It could have turned into being even more serious for Mom."

"The Chief wouldn't let anything happen to her. Even in the short time I've been around them, I can see the devotion."

"My father got to see a little bit of that devotion the other day. I don't think he appreciates it as much as the rest of us do." Foster took another small helping of the lasagna.

"Oh, I forgot about that. I think I was gone to Raleigh when that happened. I take it that he's left already."

"Yes, Simon Young doesn't like situations that don't go his way. He's my father and I love him, but sometimes I don't like him too much. He thought that a surprise visit would be well-received by everyone. He has this crazy idea that my mother would run back into his arms if he looked in her direction. Keep in mind, this is after the man has an affair with one of his employees, who is about my age, and divorces his wife of thirty-plus years to marry her. His new wife is now expecting, which wasn't part of the 'Simon Plan.' So, now he's separated from the mother of his latest child and says that he's only going to be financially supportive of this new family he's created." Foster blew out a long breath and rubbed his forehead.

"Wow! That's some story. He sounds like an interesting man." Joe shook his head, frowning.

"You can be blunter than that. He was not a bad father in any sense of the word, but it was my mother who saw to it that me and my sisters' needs were met and that we got the love, structure, and discipline we needed. It wasn't until I was in college that I fully realized how 'hands-off' he truly was."

"Foster is not exaggerating. He and I have known each other since our early high school years. We spent a lot of time together, especially our last couple of years in high school. I rarely saw Mr. Young. In fact, I still refer to him as Mr. Young because I never felt comfortable enough with him to call him Simon. I've called Foster's mother Jenn since I was sixteen." Michelle reached over, patting her husband on the arm. "I remember during our first semester away at college, something went wrong with Foster's car and it needed a serious repair. Foster didn't call his father about the situation. He called Jenn and she provided him with a solution. It's one of the reasons that Foster and I moved here, and I'm sure it's factoring into Claire's decision. We want to be closer to her so that we can continue to spend time together."

"Anyway, Dad looked at a couple of the condos that are for sale in the buildings on each side of this one. After meeting Randy, he didn't seem too interested in buying one. Dad left a little over forty-eight hours after he arrived. I think his little taste of reality might have done him some good. He now believes that Mom is in a relationship. I'm not sure if that will completely deter him from his crazy notion that he can get Mom back, but at least he understands that he has some serious competition."

"Actually, I wouldn't call Randy competition." Michelle spoke up. "Randy is in a class by himself where Jenn is concerned. She's too smart of a woman to go back to a bad situation. She gave it her all and raised three wonderful children. Now, it's her turn."

"To Aunt J's and the Chief's future!" Joe raised his glass with the other three quickly joining. "I look forward to calling him Uncle R one day! And that will be strange!"

The roar of laughter erupted around the table. Like all the time he was spending with these people he now called family, Joe felt right at home.

"I understand that the investigation and the impending trial is going to take a lot of twists and turns." Joe sat across from Neil and Renee at a small table in the kitchen of the condo he was helping to remodel. "I know that most of this will be 'a necessary evil,' so to speak, in your eyes. You've already gotten what you have been waiting for all these years."

"That's certainly true. We are still overwhelmed with happiness to have our son back." Neil squeezed Renee's hand.

"The District Attorney has told us that we do not need to attend the entire trial, but your father and I feel that it's important for us to be there to support you."

"That's part of what I'd like to talk to you about. A few days ago, I went to visit Samantha Fairfield in jail. She's being held at a location right outside of Raleigh."

Looking from Renee to Neil, Joe did not think they looked surprised by his news. Perhaps, they'd imagined that he would visit the woman at some point during her incarceration. They both remained silent, waiting for him to continue.

"After having a little time to adjust to the shock of everything and to begin to formulate my own thoughts and opinions, I had a couple of questions that I wanted to ask her. Randy advised me that if I wanted to have any contact with her, I should do so before the trial began as access to her might be limited during the trial and thereafter."

"Randy would certainly have a better understanding of those types of matters. You are wise to listen to him." Neil nodded before taking a drink of coffee. Each of them had a steaming cup.

"My visit was short and to the point. I will tell you that Samantha Fairfield is a shell of her former self. She has always been a thin person, but I can tell she's probably lost twenty pounds or more since she's been in jail. Her physical appearance makes her appear to have aged many years. I imagine that is partially because of the stress of putting up with Woodrow's abuse and keeping the secret of my identity all of these years."

Joe closed his eyes for a moment, taking a deep breath. He felt a soft hand on top of his. Opening his eyes, he saw Renee's filled with concern, and tears. Joe wondered if this seemingly strong woman, who had just fought and won a battle with cancer, ever looked as frail as Samantha. Even at the worst of her grief over him, she'd certainly never lived with an abusive husband or lied to her child. That made a difference.

"I will admit that at the beginning of learning the truth, I was concerned about her. She raised me and was one of the few people who I thought showed me genuine love. As the magnitude of the situation has begun to sink in and I've gotten a glimpse on the life I missed out on, those feelings have turned bitter."

"Those feelings are natural, son." Neil stared at Joe intently. "You would certainly care about this woman who you thought was your mother. Feeling bitter is also a logical outcome as you are getting to know your family. We are awesome!" Neil's laugh was hearty and genuine.

"I won't get into the details, but I wanted to try to get to the heart of the reason I was taken, if that was possible. Everything I've heard so far has indicated that Woodrow was certainly a criminal with a sordid history of serious crimes. I think the investigation is leaning toward him having an association with some sort of mafia or syndicate. None of it shows that he ever, before me or afterward, committed a crime against a child, such as abduction. My kidnapping was an isolated incident fueled solely by his wife's desire to have a child. The fact that I was taken might have been totally random. I was probably out of the sight of an adult for a split second and that was long enough for an experienced criminal like Woodrow to snatch me."

The happy expressions that had been on his parents' faces moments earlier were long gone. Wet streaks marked Renee's face. Neil's forehead revealed deep lines.

"I wanted to know if Samantha was involved in any way. I found out quite clearly that she was the reason a child was taken. For once, Woodrow was trying to please his wife. I also wanted to know why she hadn't tried at some point to make the situation right. It was obvious when the police initially searched the house that she knew exactly who I was, who you two are, and where I was taken from. Despite all that knowledge, she did not feel compelled to change the situation when I was young or after Woodrow was dead. In her eyes, I belonged to her. Even if she could have gone back and did things differently, she would not have. She was not willing to return the kidnapped child to his biological family. Even my attending from the police academy and moving closer to where I'd been taken didn't wake up her conscience. Samantha Fairfield put her desire to have a child before that child's right to know who he was and be raised by his rightful parents. She has no remorse."

"That must have been a hard conversation to have. We are proud of you for taking the brave steps to find out what you needed to know." Neil's voice was strong but filled with emotion.

All the support that he continually felt from Neil and Renee, and all his extended family and friends was overwhelming for Joe. He knew it was what was fueling his healing and making him stronger.

"In the interest of my mental health going forward, in order to rebuild my life, and out of respect for the two people who *never* gave up on me, I believe the best decision is for me to sever all ties with Samantha Fairfield. I will, of course, appear in court to testify and cooperate fully with whatever the investigation needs. I will not sit in the courtroom in support of her. I cannot be a witness for the defense. I cannot condone a lifetime of lies and secrets."

"Oh, Jonah, Joe." Renee's voice broke. "I know that is a difficult decision for you. Please know that we will continue to love and support you no matter what you decide to do regarding Samantha Fairfield. We do not expect you to completely forget she existed. Your father and I may never be able to forgive the heartache she and her husband caused us, but we can appreciate the care she gave to you, no matter her motives."

"I realize that. I don't suppose I can honestly say that I will never reach out to her again. 'Never' can be a long or short time. At this point though, I do not desire to remain in contact with someone whose love for me had conditions. All those conditions were based on lies and withholding things in my life that were rightfully mine. I don't want to be bitter. I think focusing on what's ahead, instead of what is behind me, is the best way to cultivate good mental health."

"How did you get to be so wise, Joe?" Neil reached over, patting Joe on the shoulder.

"Honestly, this realization comes from some long heart-to-heart conversations with Randy. He seems to know what I need to hear."

"Our family is so fortunate to have him in our lives." Renee shook her head, affirmatively. "I never realized when he stepped back into Jenn's life, what a positive effect he could have on all of us."

"I could call him the uncle I never had, except that I'm hoping that won't be a true statement for too much longer."

CHAPTER NINE

Rachel

"Have you heard any more from Ross since he visited?" Doris took a long drink of her coffee in the sunroom of Rachel's house.

"Yes, we've had a couple of short phone calls. Ross is planning to come visit again soon and, perhaps, stay for a couple of days."

"That sounds lovely. I assume this means he would like to have some sort of relationship with you?"

"I think so. At least, he wants to get to know me better and learn more about his father."

"Understandable pursuits for someone who is adopted. Has he said why he waited so late in his life to seek his birth parents?"

"His adoption was never a secret in his family. His parents were quite open about his origins. Ross has indicated that he didn't have much desire to find us until after both of his parents passed. The records regarding his adoption were sealed. He had no idea that he had a way of finding out my name until he found his original birth certificate in his mother's belongings after she died. Mrs. Lancaster had kept it."

"That was fortunate for both you and Ross."

"I believe that women are, by nature, keepers. Women keep their secrets tucked away. Sometimes a woman keeps a secret so long that she forgets she has it. That may be the case with Mrs. Lancaster. Perhaps she meant to give Ross that piece of information at some point. Time and circumstance may have altered that memory."

"It's a gift. A gift that both you and Ross can unwrap together. Telling him the story of your relationship with Jordan has stirred the dust on some old memories, I presume."

"It has. It's made me wonder what happened to him. If this relationship had occurred in today's world, I would have been able to keep up with him for the rest of his life, to some extent. The internet would have helped me do that."

"I've been thinking about that very thing. It's one of the reasons I came by today. Would you like me to use my internet skills to see what I can find out about Jordan's life?"

"If you had asked me that question a month ago, I would have said no. I would have spouted some feelings-hiding excuse about leaving the past in the past. That Rachel would have said that she gave Jordan up the moment she gave her baby boy to another mother."

"What does Rachel today say?"

"She realizes that Ross has the right to know something about the kind of man his father was. I only knew Jordan for a few months. That's only a fraction of time to know who he really was."

"The internet can reveal a wealth of information, if any of Jordan's life is recorded online. If not, it can provide us some stepping stones to additional ways to learn more. You know, there are benefits to working for a newspaper. One of the best investigative reporters I've ever known has an office only a few feet from my desk."

"Since I know that Jenn has only recently rejoined the newspaper industry, I'm going to presume you are not referring to her. Keep in mind that she doesn't know my secret."

"I understand. I was referring to Lyle Livingston. Lyle could find a needle in a haystack. He also has an alibi to give him clout when it comes to asking questions."

"Alibi? You make it sound like he would be committing a crime. It's not a crime to try and find something out about a person's life, especially a person who is probably deceased."

"I know. It's the only word I could think of to use. Lyle could make phone calls and ask questions on the premise of being a reporter, because he is one."

"That's true. I'd rather that my secret life did not become fodder for one of Lyle's deep and interesting articles though."

"You have aptly described Lyle's stories. I do think though that Lyle also has a helping nature. I believe he could be persuaded to do some investigative work 'on the side,' so to speak. I think he would use his skills to help a friend to learn some truths."

"I'm not ashamed of what happened. Especially after meeting this wonderful man who I had a part in creating. I wouldn't mind shouting it from the rooftops or the front page of the *Serendipity Sun*, but it's not only my story to tell. This is Ross' life, his story."

"That's a discussion for a different day. Who knows how Ross may feel once he has a clearer picture of everything that transpired and who you and Jordan are and were. In the meantime, I could do a little digging, with or without Lyle's help, and see what interesting tidbits might be revealed."

"Be my guest. Knowing your tenacity, I'm not sure that I could stop you anyway." Rachel gave her friend a knowing smile behind her laugh. "I know you have my best interests at heart. That's all that matters."

"Always." Doris looked at her watch. "Our chats make me lose track of time. I've got to be at a church committee meeting in forty-five minutes. Help me remember that."

"You are asking the wrong person to help you remember. I'll be eighty-five soon. What's new at the office?"

"The new real estate promotion project that Jenn's daughter-in-law, Michelle, is working on with Betsy and Ellie is going gangbusters. I believe it is going to make a significant impact on the newspaper's bottom line at it continues to develop. That's exciting. We are also doing something fun in-house this weekend. Jenn would like to do a little interior remodeling—a fresh coat of paint and a little sprucing up. We had her office painted before she arrived. Lyle painted his office during his first week back. It gave Jenn an idea to do it throughout the whole building. On Friday, we are closing the office at noon. Everyone is going to change into painting clothes, and we are going to repaint all the offices. Then have a dinner afterward. In a few weeks, during the night of the Christmas parade, we will have an open house. It will be a great way to introduce Jenn, and many other new folks on our team, to the people of Serendipity."

"That's a fabulous idea. I bet there are many who haven't been in the newspaper office in years, especially with everything that can be done online now."

"Exactly! We also thought it would be a nice way to get some of our clients into the office as well. They can see where our product is made. Meet some of the behind-the-scenes folks who aren't as well-known in the public but play a vital role in the newspaper's production each week."

"I imagine that will be advertised in some of the future issues, but please make sure I get that date on my calendar."

"Absolutely! I believe the parade is on the first Saturday in December. I will double check though and let you know."

"A painting party! How fun! I hope it is catered by that delightful company that provided the lunch Jenn brought me the other day. I know they have a clever name, but, for the life of me, I can never remember it."

"More Please. Yes, that is who will be providing the food for Friday evening. They are hands down the best caterer in this town."

"The food was delightful. I enjoyed visiting with Jenn. I believe that her mother's passing has made her realize that we often know less about those closest to us than we imagine. I recall having that feeling after my parents passed. Perhaps you did the same."

"I did. You go through your life thinking that you know your mother and father better than anyone in the world. Then, they pass, and you reflect on their lives realizing that your knowledge of them is tainted with your own viewpoint. As you mentioned earlier in this conversation, I found secrets in my mother's belongings. They remained secrets because by then I had no one to ask about them."

"Paisley and I found a photo of a young man in our mother's belongings. The inscription on the back spoke of promises of everlasting love and the man's first name—Rhett. Neither of us ever saw the photo while our mother was alive. None of Mother's siblings or friends were left. She took that secret with her."

"I daresay that every person who has ever lived dies with knowledge in their heart which they never share with another soul. It's a happy and a sad thought."

"It is. It indeed is."

"I was surprised to receive your call this morning, Amber. I didn't realize that you'd returned to Serendipity so soon."

On her way to a follow-up appointment with her oncologist at the Cancer Center, Renee dropped off Amber for a visit with their aunt. Rachel said a silent prayer that Renee would continue to get a miraculous cancer-free report from her doctors.

"Willis was settled back in his school routine. Dawson has tons of work to catch up on. I thought that was my cue to take a weekday flight back to the East Coast."

"Darling girl, we've been so worried about you." Rachel reached across the table where they were drinking tea, taking Amber's hands in her own.

"I know, Aunt Rachel. I'm sorry for all the worry and heartache I've caused my family. Mom's passing put me in a tailspin. My weaknesses took over."

"Grief has the power to reach inside us and take over who we are. Grief that comes to us in a shocking way doubles its intensity and power over our actions. From what I have heard about your treatment, this time your doctors seem to have applied cutting edge principles that also put some of the success and control of your recovery in your own hands. I am amazed that you have been prescribed a drug that will help you overcome a drug substance of another kind."

"I know. Many people think that is a foolish approach." Amber lowered her head.

"I am not one of them. I think it's like beating the drug at its own game. I asked Mr. Google about it and did some of my own reading when Renee or Jenn shared this treatment plan with me. I understand that you will not be on the medication forever. It makes sense that you could overcome an addiction more effectively when it is a gradual process. I think the real key is that you will be in control of your own treatment while you are back in the 'real world,' so to speak, and no longer in a rehab facility. With your loving family surrounding you and giving you empowerment, it should be nothing but successful."

"I knew I needed to spend some time with you. I have always been able to count on my Aunt Rachel to say the things I need to hear, whether I wanted to hear them or not." Amber's expression changed from solemn to smiling. "Today, you are saying exactly what I needed to hear."

"Your son is quickly growing into a handsome young man, like his father. How is he weathering this storm in your life?"

"Willis has a personality and temperament almost identical to that of his father's. Dawson is strong and disciplined."

"I suppose that would be from his successful career in sports. I always get this wrong. Did he play football?"

"No. He was a basketball player. Dawson was a star athlete in high school, college, and eventually with the NBA. That stands for the National Basketball Association. Age would have caught up with him eventually. If it hadn't been for a car accident that messed up his knees, I think he might still be playing professionally. That life is what has made him so disciplined. He has taught Willis to be that way."

"I hear a lot of love in your voice in regard to Dawson."

"I've loved him from the first moment I met him."

"Was your divorce a hasty decision then?"

"Plain and simple, the divorce was a byproduct of the addiction. I pushed Dawson's love away. I thought he would be better off without me."

"His love for you is strong as well."

"His love for me is stronger than the both of us. Dawson has never once given up on me. He hated getting divorced. Looking back, I think he knew that it had to be part of the process. For me to see things clearly, I had to lose some of the aspects of my life which were the most important. You know that my relationship with my mother was challenging. Despite being the baby of the family, Mom didn't spoil me."

"Your father was another story."

"Yes, there is no doubt that I was a spoiled Daddy's girl. Mom and I, however, were like oil and water during most of my growing up years. I think that she could see that I was going to have challenges later in life."

"You are wiser than you give yourself credit for, my dear. That is exactly what Paisley thought. She told me several times that your personality was not going to allow you to have an easy life. You would go looking for the hard way."

Rachel watched the young woman twirl her finger in her hair. No doubt, an unconscious habit from Amber's younger years.

"She was right. I think that is one of the factors in her sudden passing that sent me spiraling. Mom worked hard to prepare me to face challenges head-on. She spent time individually and collectively molding her three daughters into becoming strong women. We could see who she wanted us to be by watching you and her, and earlier, Grammie Elana."

"Strong women breed strong women. It's what allows our species to continue." Rachel stared at the fragile, yet resilient, young woman before her. How proud Paisley would be of all her daughters.

"Enough about me. I believe that you have a birthday coming up soon. I remember the New Year's Eve birthday parties you used to host here when my sisters and I were growing up. How old will you be on this one?"

"Ah, my dear, you know it's not nice to ask a lady her age."

"Unless it is a lady whom you know is proud to flaunt her years on this planet. Do tell, Aunt Rachel."

The sweet, angelic smile Rachel remembered from Amber's early years crossed the face of her beloved niece. It touched Rachel's heart. Many fervent prayers had been uttered on the young woman's behalf. Rachel fondly remembered the long afternoon visits Amber would make in her early teens. Amber took many years of piano from a teacher who lived one block from Rachel's home. Paisley would drop her daughter off with instructions to visit her aunt when the lesson was over. Those were special times between the two that Rachel missed when Amber grew old enough to drive herself.

"Do you still play the piano?" Rachel allowed her thoughts to verbalize.

"My goodness! What made you think of that?" Amber smiled, glancing in the direction of the piano in the next room that could barely be seen through the edge of the doorway. "I do not play often. I do try to stretch my fingers over the keys a few times a year to ensure that my parents' investment on my musical training does not disappear. We have a piano in our home in California. I've tried to get Willis interested in music."

"You will have to visit me often and help keep our heirloom family piano in tune. Seriously, I would ask Paisley to sit down at it once a year to determine if I needed to contact a tuner."

"It would be my pleasure. I sat down at the piano in California a few days ago and found the experience to be cathartic in a way I have never felt before."

"Interesting."

"You've sidetracked me away from my question about your birthday. Are you going to make me resort to consulting with Doris?"

"Pfft. I have no issues with my age. Proud to have lived to call it my own. I shall be eighty-five years young on December 31. I expect a party."

Rachel watched Amber's eyes bug out in surprise.

"I do not want it to be a surprise. I want plenty of time to plan my wardrobe and have a long beauty nap in the hours prior to the event. I must look my best."

Amber's shocked expression turned to laughing, shaking her head.

"My nieces are not sly enough to pull off a surprise for me. Extend me the same courtesy you will give the guests, send me a 'save the date' card."

Before Amber could respond, Rachel heard the front door open and Renee's voice announcing her entrance.

"I'm back! What are you two chatting about?"

"My birthday party that will not be a surprise."

Renee gave Amber a wide-eyed look when she reached the room.

"Don't blame your little sister. I smelled a surprise in the works a couple of weeks ago. You can thank Doris for my suspicions." Rachel shook her head, frowning. "As well as that woman knows me, she asked if I was going to attend a New Year's Eve party."

"Aunt Rachel, what makes you think that your darling nieces were planning anything?" Renee batted her eyes, sitting down next to Amber.

"Ouch!" Amber screeched, swatting Renee's fingers away from the side of her thigh.

"Leave your sister alone, Renee. She did not reveal anything. I did instruct her that I do not wish to have a surprise party. I want a party that I can plan for, including having the necessary rest prior to the event so that I can 'party' until the ball drops or all the candles burn out on my cake, whichever comes first."

"Okay, Aunt Rachel, we can accommodate that request. We will be having your not-a-surprise party on the evening of December 31."

"Shocking!" Rachel rolled her eyes. "Have you chosen a location?"

Rachel watched the sisters make eye contact.

"Well, that's sort of a long story. Perhaps, we better wait until Jenn is with us before we explain."

"Please do not feel like you must go to a great expense by renting some grand location like one of those places that hold big weddings. I know that's big business in these coastal towns."

"It's not a matter of expense." Renee reached over and took Rachel's hand. "We would spare no expense for our beloved aunt, our second mother."

Instantly, Rachel felt her eyes fill with tears. Her heart swelled with love for the daughters of her dear Paisley.

"It is a special location. We cannot reveal it to you at this time. Jenn needs to be here so that we can tell you a secret that we have been keeping."

"I love secrets, especially when they are not about me." Rachel pulled both girls into a strong embrace. "You are my heart, dear girls. I look forward to hearing your secret."

"I didn't expect to see you again so soon, Renee." Rachel opened her front door on the following day. "I was distressed with myself after you and Amber left yesterday when I realized that we got all caught up with silly birthday party talk and did not discuss your doctor's appointment."

"No worries, Aunt Rachel. I would much rather discuss your party than anything related to cancer or doctors. Rest your weary heart. The check-up reaffirmed that love is the most powerful drug of all. My cancer remains in remission. I do not have to go back to the doctor for six months. Hurrah!"

"That is wonderful news!"

"The reason I stopped by was to bring a menu from the caterer we plan to use for your party. Jenn says that you are familiar with the company. They have a quite clever name."

"More Please. I don't often remember the name, but Doris and I discussed them the other day while she was telling me about an event they are having at the newspaper."

"Yes! I haven't had the opportunity to taste their food, but everyone raves about it." Renee handed Rachel a folder. "Since you are part of the planning committee now, we thought it made sense for you to assist with the menu choices."

"That would be lovely. You will consider them as ideas and suggestions. The true party planners should make the final decisions." Rachel set the folder down on the table next to her chair. "Since the conversation you and I had a few days ago, I've been thinking about the woman who raised Jonah."

Rachel watched Renee's relaxed expression change to a pained one. Rachel wanted her niece to know that she understood the pain that was in Renee's heart. It was time.

"Our lives have been similar, yours and mine. The circumstances have been different as has been the span of time. Like you, I was a mother without a child. A child who was taken from my arms because of a situation I could not control. It would be over sixty years before I would see my son again."

Renee gasped. Her eyes grew large. Tears ran down her face.

"What? How?"

"Sit back, my dear. I'm going to share a secret that only a few people knew when it happened and even fewer know now. I have a story."

CHAPTER TEN

Renee

"JENN, I ASKED NEIL to invite Randy out to dinner tonight so that you, Amber, and I could have some time alone."

"Renee, I don't like the tone of your voice. You told us last night that everything was fine with your tests." Jenn glanced from Renee to Amber. "Is something wrong?"

"No, Jenn. I was completely truthful with you. The doctors say that I am fine." Renee took a deep breath. "I dropped off the catering menus to Aunt Rachel this morning, as we discussed. She decided to tell me a secret. I'm dumbfounded with shock. She poured her heart out to me."

"We've discussed several times through the years that there was something about Aunt Rachel we didn't know." Jenn leaned back in her chair, a feeling of relief washing over her.

"She has always been so bold and daring." Amber's eyes darted from side-to-side. "Maybe she fell in love with a married man who wouldn't leave his wife."

"Another true statement." Standing in the doorway to the living room, Renee looked over her shoulder.

Amber gasped. Jenn bit her bottom lip while she grimaced.

"That isn't the saddest part of her story. Aunt Rachel told me that I could tell you two all that she shared with me this afternoon. I told her that would not satisfy my sisters, especially one who has always told a 'story' of some sort for a living. She was going to have to come here and tell it herself."

Renee could hear movement in the hallway. A few seconds later, her beloved aunt walked around her and entered the living room.

"Three Halston sisters in one room, it is a wonderful sight for these old eyes." Aunt Rachel patted Renee on the back as she walked by. "Has the oldest in this trio advised you two to put on your seatbelts?"

Renee snorted in laughter, watching the expressions on her sisters' faces. It was almost like her mother calling a family meeting to share some dreaded piece of news, like someone was cancelling Christmas because report cards were not acceptable.

"I'm going to make some strong coffee whilst you recount what you shared with me. I will be in the kitchen cooking a delicious dinner as your reward for your storytelling labors."

"I hope it is a meal of comfort food."

"How does Paisley's Pot Pie sound with bacon-braised Brussel sprouts and homemade hush puppies?"

"My sister's seafood pot pie would be heavenly. I shall be certain to tell my tales with dramatic flourish to earn this food reward."

"Don't get too dramatic, Aunt Rachel." Renee continued walking into the living room with her aunt, helping her be seated. "They've had their own firsthand experiences with drama of late."

"What is it with this family?" Jenn shook her head. "Every generation seems to have some sort of interesting saga."

"My dear, I'd like to say our family was unique in that situation." Aunt Rachel sat down in the most comfortable chair in the living room. "There are plenty of families, famous and unknown, who would be stiff competition. Have you heard of the Kennedys? Or maybe the name Presley rings a bell?"

"Touché, Aunt Rachel." Amber nodded in agreement. "Those basketball wives I became friends with made most soap operas look tame."

A few minutes later, after preparing coffee for them, Renee reentered the living room to find Aunt Rachel deep into the story about her first love, Richard Bergman.

"This is the engagement ring Richard gave me. Come here, Renee, you didn't get to see this earlier."

Renee stood next to where her aunt was sitting, peering over the woman's shoulder as Aunt Rachel reached into a small silk bag that had a flower design on burgundy fabric. The ring that emerged from the bag had a large pear-shaped emerald stone encircled in small diamonds.

"That is beautiful. Is there a significance to the emerald?" Renee took the ring from Aunt Rachel's hands, examining it more closely. The band was small. It only fit on Renee's pinkie.

"Richard was born in May. Emerald was his birthstone. This ring belonged to his grandmother. Her birthday was also in May." Rachel took the ring back from Renee, handing it to Jenn. "I offered to give it back to Richard's family. They told me that Richard had given it to me, so it was mine. I wore it faithfully for many years until my fingers got too large for it to fit comfortably."

"I must confess that Aunt Rachel told me this story not long ago while I was visiting her one day. I didn't get to see this beautiful ring though." Jenn handed the ring to Amber. "I did get to see the photograph of a handsome young man. It was in that big album sitting on the coffee table."

"It is, Jenn. Please hand it to me. Don't give all the story away though."

Jenn handed the old photograph album to Aunt Rachel. Renee watched the woman turn each page, pausing to look at some of the photos along the way. Soon, she was in the middle of the book gazing upon a sepia photograph of a young soldier.

"This is Richard. I can still remember the first day he came to pick me up for a date. I was barely sixteen. He had made visits to my home during the year prior, but Father would not allow me to go anywhere with him until I was sixteen. This photo is the first one that was taken of him in the military." Rachel stroked the photo, lovingly. "My mind cannot imagine what he would have looked like as an older man. My heart holds him just like this photograph. If we'd only had recording devices then like are available today. Richard had a beautiful voice. He was a fine singer. We would often take long walks through the neighborhood with Richard serenading me with whatever was the latest song of the day."

"He's very handsome, Aunt Rachel." Amber moved closer to stand on the other side of Aunt Rachel's chair. "What color were his eyes? Is his hair dark?"

"His hair was jet black; so black it almost had a blue sheen. It was lovely with his crystal blue eyes. As you can see, Richard was quite handsome. He had a movie star handsomeness to him. He was humble though. Richard had no idea how good looking he was."

Aunt Rachel pointed to several more photos of him before turning to a page that included several casual and posed photos of the two of them, sweetheart photos.

"Look how young you are!" Amber pointed to a photo of Richard pushing Aunt Rachel on a swing. They were both laughing.

"We had so much fun before he went into the Army. His leave times were shorter and less frequent as his years of service continued. Richard always seemed to be halfway around the world. It got harder for him to come home."

"Did you ever wish that Gramps and Grammie would have allowed you to marry Richard at a younger age?" Jenn verbalized the question that was in Renee's heart.

"Sometimes. I've wondered if things would have turned out differently if we'd been married and I was able to go overseas with him. I don't think that his job duties would have changed. Richard enjoyed being a courier. It was one of the safer jobs to have, except when it wasn't. When I told Jenn this story the other day, she talked about my grieving the loss of an 'almost husband.' I've thought about that term since and how applicable it is. I don't think that I was able to mourn Richard properly. Even though he had been in my life since I was fifteen, I was probably nineteen or twenty before I really felt 'in love' with him. He was four years older than me. Richard fell in love from the beginning. In the years since he's been gone, I've continued to love him, partially because of the guilt I felt that I didn't love him enough while he was here. I can honestly say that I've thought about him every day, sending him a little love in the hopes that it somehow continues to reach his heart."

Renee's eyes were filled with tears. Her sisters' eyes glistened as well.

"Thank you for sharing that with us, Aunt Rachel. That is a special story." Amber leaned over the chair from behind, hugging Aunt Rachel.

"I kept in touch with Richard's parents for the rest of their short lives. Both died younger than they should have, no doubt from broken hearts from not knowing whatever happened to their only son. I worried so much about Renee and Neil all the years that our dear Jonah was missing. Not knowing can be worse than the dreaded truth."

"I understand that perfectly, Aunt Rachel." Renee wiped tears from her eyes. "I wish that Richard's parents could have had some sort of closure.

"Indeed, my dear. It would have been a blessing. I'm afraid that the guilt that this young girl carried fueled my impetuous nature and caused me to act out of character in the years shortly after."

"Would that be our cue to the second secret of your life?" Jenn flipped ahead in the old photo album which was sitting on her lap.

"I'm afraid that my real secrets do not come with photographs or trinkets of love. Richard might have been a secret to you, but he was not a secret to anyone of that time. There are only a handful of people, living and dead, who know about the other two loves of my life. No pictures honor our union."

"Before you dive into this story, let's move into the dining room. I believe our food is ready."

With the help of her sisters, Renee moved the entrée and side dishes to the dining room table. Each with their chosen beverage, the four women took a spot at the large table and began to eat.

"This is just as I remember it." Amber took a second bite of the pot pie. "It's so full of seafood goodness and that rich sauce. You've nailed Mom's dish, Renee. I'm so glad this food memory is preserved."

"Are you girls aware that your mother created this recipe?" Aunt Rachel took a small bite of hush puppy before she continued. "Early in your mother's cooking experience, Paisley found that pies were one of her specialties. Your father did not seem to mind their frequent appearance on the dinner table, so she began adapting a basic chicken pot pie recipe to include other creative ingredients. This seafood pie took what could always be abundantly found in Serendipity, an assortment of different types of seafood, and made it into a staple in this family. Our mother helped Paisley perfect that luscious cream sauce in this house's original kitchen. It is indeed a dish of love and heritage."

"Mom told me some of that story when she taught me how to make it." Renee spooned another small serving of the dish onto her own plate. "I don't recall her mentioning that Grammie Elana was involved in its creation. That would explain the sherry that is included in the sauce."

"I found Grammie Elana's collection of recipes when I first moved in." Jenn helped herself to more of the dish. "I was amazed at how many of her recipes included sherry."

"Sherry was our mother's answer to any problem." Aunt Rachel chuckled. "I remember first tasting the strong beverage when I was in my first year of primary school. I was sick with a horrendous cold and a hacking cough that would not quit. Whatever medicine the doctor prescribed was not doing its job. Mom had me drink a jigger of sherry. I was asleep in no time. When I awoke, my cough had diminished considerably."

"Mom actually drank sherry to keep a cough away." Renee laughed, looking at the special sherry glasses that were sitting in the corner glass cabinet behind Jenn. "I remember when Jonah was three, he had a horrible case of croup. Mom and Dad drove to Raleigh to check on us. She brought a large cooler full of homemade food and a new bottle of sherry. She gave Jonah a small sip from a juice glass. He went right to sleep and rested for almost the whole night." Renee reflected on the memory.

"Continue telling us stories from your youth, Aunt Rachel. We must know all the secrets."

The anxious look on Amber's face reminded Renee of how much her youngest sister loved hearing someone tell a story. The considerable age difference between the two of them resulted in Renee often having the responsibility of being left in charge of Amber. Every week, Renee would walk Amber to the public library that was only a few blocks from their

Danner Street home. Amber would be so excited when they would arrive to find the sign out indicating that 'Storybook Lady' was reading a story. Amber would hang on every word until the end.

"Very well. You must allow for interruptions as I finish this delightful meal. I'm a slower eater than I once was." Aunt Rachel took a small bite of the pie, chewing carefully for a few moments before she swallowed with a drink of water. "As I said earlier, I was filled with guilt after Richard disappeared in a land far away. Despite the prodding of many of my teacher friends, I could not be persuaded to go on any dates that were offered to me. I committed myself to my work, taking all sorts of advanced courses in the hopes of eventually becoming a school administrator. I decided to take off one summer though. It would be a time that changed my life."

Jenn's phone buzzed on the table beside her. Everyone was so intently listening to Aunt Rachel that they jumped at the sound.

"I'm sorry. It's Emily. She rarely calls during the week; I better take it."

While Jenn stepped into another room, Renee and Amber gathered the dishes from the table. Aunt Rachel continued finishing her meal. Renee put the leftovers into containers, carefully packing a special box of goodies for Aunt Rachel. Amber quickly loaded the dishwasher.

"I'll pour everyone a fresh glass of iced tea." Amber carried a pitcher of tea and four glasses into the living room.

"Sorry for the delay. Emily is debating between job offers and entering law school." Jenn joined them in the living room.

"I know that you were concerned that the topic of law school seemed to come out of nowhere. Have you found out anything further regarding its origin?" Renee handed Jenn a glass of tea.

"Foster says that Emily began talking about law school months ago. Maybe around the time that Mom passed. He said that she'd quietly applied to several schools and has been accepted to at least two. She never took a break between completing her undergraduate degree and entering graduate school. It's hard to imagine Emily having even more years of education ahead."

"One can become burned out from studying too long." Aunt Rachel spoke up from her comfortable chair near the front window.

"We shall see what she decides. Emily is a planner. I'm sure she's looked at all possibilities. Please continue your story, Aunt Rachel."

"I was in my mid-twenties when I took a summer off to stay with my Aunt Ardelia in a small town on the coast of South Carolina. Ardelia was a Frederick, the oldest sister of my father. Her husband, Uncle Henry, had passed earlier the same year."

"I think I remember hearing about us having a Great-Aunt Ardelia." Renee furrowed her brow remembering. "Do we know some of her descendants?"

"Sadly, we do not. Ardelia and Henry had one son, Frederick. He was given Ardelia's family name. Frederick was a few years older than me. I don't remember all the details, but Fred passed in his thirties in a tragic accident. His wife and young daughter moved out West where she was from. She remarried and we lost touch." Aunt Rachel took a long drink of tea. "I took the train from Raleigh to Charleston to visit Aunt Ardelia that summer. She lived in a small community that was about an hour's drive from the city. Her next-door neighbor worked in Charleston. She asked him to pick me up at the train station on his way home from work. His name was Jordan Rivers."

"Here we go, girls, the story is starting." Amber pulled her legs up on the couch, forming a ball of comfort.

"Jordan was a lawyer in a successful practice. He was in his late thirties. Despite the age difference, we had a lively conversation on the drive from Charleston. He was different from anyone I had ever met. All the young men whom I had dated up until that point, even Richard, were quite one-dimensional. They could converse about topics that interested them or the popular sports of the day. None of them seemed to know much about the news of the world and certainly not literature or theatre. Jordan had a wicked sense of humor. He'd traveled the world while in college. He was up to date on the politics of the day, not only in this country, but in key parts of the world. By the time we reached the driveway that he shared with my aunt's home, I was head over heels for Jordan. He opened my door and took my hand to help me out of the car. It was a moment that was straight out of a movie. It was magic."

Rachel spent the next half hour telling them more about that summer with Jordan. From the trips to Charleston to the few days when Aunt Ardelia was out of town.

"You are probably shocked to learn that your spinster aunt had an affair with a married man. While not totally unexpected, it was frowned upon in that time. It would have never happened if I'd known from the beginning that Jordan was married. My aunt never mentioned it when she told me about the person who would be picking me up at the train station. Jordan never spoke of his wife during our drive to my aunt's home. Jordan didn't tell me about his wife until he began to speak of her being in a sanitarium because of the mental state that resulted from the multiple miscarriages. By then, I was in over my head. He mentioned divorcing her because her mental health was deteriorating rapidly, and she was not responding to any of the treatments. I honestly thought that Jordan and I would have a future together. I would never have let the relationship go so far physically, and emotionally, otherwise."

"Since we never had an Uncle Jordan, I'm going to assume that we are about to hear another tragic, unhappy ending." Jenn rubbed her forehead, frowning.

"No one died this time, at least not physically. It was more heartbreaking though, at least for me."

Aunt Rachel took a deep breath, staring off into space for a while before she resumed speaking. Renee made brief eye contact with each of her sisters. Like her, they seemed to be holding their breath. Even though Renee knew how the story would end, it did not change her heart racing in anticipation of hearing it.

"After my aunt returned from her trip, Jordan began spending more nights in Charleston than he did at his home. I thought, perhaps, he was ashamed of what had transpired between us. I knew that I would soon be returning home, so I tried to start putting Jordan out of my mind. I took a taxi to the train station for my return trip home."

"Oh, I was so hoping for one of those happy endings like we've seen on old black-and-white movies." Amber sniffled, wiping her nose.

"This story is far from over, my dear girl. Keep listening." Aunt Rachel took out a tissue that was tucked in the pocket of her lightweight sweater. "I was overcome with emotion while I sat on the train waiting for it to depart. I had a window seat. As the train began to pull away, I glanced at the platform and saw Jordan standing there. Our eyes met. He blew me a kiss. I waved until I could no longer see him."

"Oh, that is just like a movie." Jenn spoke through her tears. "Jordan loved you. He came to say goodbye."

"That might have been the end of this story if something else hadn't have happened a couple of weeks later." Again, Aunt Rachel took a deep breath, shaking her head. "For about a week, I was sick each morning before I even had my breakfast. Naively, I thought I had a virus of some sort."

Amber gasped, covering her mouth.

"Finally, I went to the doctor and was shocked to learn what my symptoms were concealing."

"Oh, no. Did something happen to that baby?" The topic was obviously making Amber upset, tears ran down her face.

"Jordan couldn't marry you. He was already married. That would be a major complication." Jenn's tone was stoic.

"Who is telling this story?" Aunt Rachel scowled.

"I'm sorry." Jenn quickly replied. "We will stop interrupting."

"The situation was indeed complicated. It was time for the school year to start. I needed to be back in a classroom here. I couldn't run back to Aunt Ardelia's without a reason. I called Jordan at his office. He was cheerful and friendly until I revealed my reason for calling. Saying little else, he told me that he would travel to Serendipity the following Saturday. The next three days trudged by at a snail's pace."

Aunt Rachel took another drink of her tea. The three sisters dared not speak.

"I had not told my parents anything about Jordan, including his impending arrival on Saturday. He called when he arrived in Serendipity. I met him at the park near the library. When I found him sitting on a bench, he looked way older than the man I'd fallen in love with a few weeks earlier. I told him about being sick and going to the doctor. He was silent for a few minutes before he finally spoke. His words were shocking. I could not believe what I was hearing."

Renee knew how the story was going to end. It hurt to see the hopeful expressions on her sisters' faces. They were still hoping for a happy ending.

"Jordan's tone was somber as he told me that he'd talked to a lawyer from another firm who specialized in adoptions. He said that there were countless couples who desperately wanted a child and would welcome the chance to adopt one. It could all be handled easily. The word 'easily' hung in the air between us. There was nothing *easy* about the situation we were in, especially for me. I was stunned. I could not believe what I was hearing. I'd only had a few days to think about the situation, but I had not considered any other alternative except having the child and being its mother."

"He would not leave his wife." Renee covered her mouth, realizing that she'd said the statement aloud.

"I would say that 'could not' was a more appropriate statement, considering what I was about to learn. During those weeks before our child was conceived, the doctors had begun a new treatment regimen on Jordan's wife, trying a new medication on her. Initially, it appeared to make her mental condition worse. The doctors adjusted the dosage, and she began to respond. A month prior, Jordan and his wife had a conjugal visit at the hospital. Mrs. Rivers was pregnant. Unlike previous times, the pregnancy was progressing normally. Her mental state made a miraculous improvement. Jordan had to take care of his wife and child, the legal versions. In his mind, there was no other alternative."

Aunt Rachel sat in silence for several minutes, staring straight ahead, lost in thought. No one dared to interrupt her journey.

"The rest of that day was a blur of tears and raised voices. Jordan accompanied me to my parents' house and faced the wrath of Carson Frederick. Jordan took all the blame, explaining how the relationship between us had developed. Telling my father that he was a weak man, distraught and lonely because of the condition of his wife. He told the story of his wife, the children they had lost, her mental state, and how the situation had recently changed. It was hard for me to stomach. I felt like a mistake."

"I'm trying to imagine how Gramps and Grammie reacted?" Jenn made eye contact with Renee.

"Mother cried. I did not feel disappointment from her, but I did see fear in her eyes. Fear of what might become of me. In my father's eyes was rage. If we'd left him alone with Jordan, I'm not sure what might have happened. The businessman in him agreed with the choice of adoption. His gentle father side was suffering. His heart was breaking. Jordan and my father handled the main details with Jordan's lawyer friend. I went back to teaching school and was able to conceal my pregnancy until it was time for Christmas Break. I asked for a leave of absence until the next school year the following fall. I stayed in an apartment in Charleston that was paid for by the adoptive parents. It was an easy pregnancy with no medical problems."

Renee looked at her sisters. Tears were pouring down their faces. This was their cousin they were learning about. As close as their mothers were, this child would have been like a sibling to them.

"My son was born in a hospital in Charleston. I held him for a few minutes after he was born. I left the hospital a couple of days later, without him. I did not meet the adoptive parents. Jordan assured my father that they were upstanding people who longed for a child."

Aunt Rachel's face was also covered with tears. Renee knew that feeling. Hers came from totally different circumstances, but she knew what it was like to think you were never going to see your child again. It was like the grief of death, only somehow worse.

"Did you ever see Jordan again?" Amber's question jarred everyone from their momentary fog.

"I did not hear from him during those months I was living in Charleston. While there, my mother told me that Aunt Ardelia had mentioned that the 'nice couple' next door had brought home a beautiful baby girl." Aunt Rachel took a deep breath. "Again, I took the train home. Looking out the window, as the train pulled away, I saw Jordan standing on the platform. Tears were streaming down his face. Guilt? Remorse? True sadness for the loss of his child, or even for the loss of me? I don't know his reasons for the emotion I saw that day. My emotional well was dry by that point. The night after my son's birth, I cried more tears than I ever had before or have since. I never heard from Jordan again. The following year, Aunt Ardelia told my mother that the Rivers moved away. I'm sure Jordan is dead by now. He would be close to one hundred, if he is not."

"I don't suppose that you ever tried to find your son. I understand that it's hard to dig up the records of a closed adoption." Jenn dried her eyes before taking a drink of tea.

"I did not. Part of the adoption agreement included a statement that I would not seek to have contact with my son or his family. My heart found comfort in my hope that he was indeed in a family that loved him unconditionally and would raise him to be a fine man."

"It would be wonderful to meet him though." Renee's tears were still coming. "It would be like my reunion with Jonah."

"That's one of the reasons why I wanted to tell all three of you my story." Aunt Rachel smiled. There was a glimmer in her eyes. "My son has recently contacted me."

Renee, Jenn, and Amber all gasped in unison.

"That's wonderful!" Amber was the first to voice their excitement.

"It is indeed. Jenn, you will be amazed to know that he came into the newspaper office to look through the newspaper obituaries."

"Oh, my! The obituaries?"

"Yes, I suppose he wanted to rule out the worst-case scenario before he spent a lot of time looking for someone who was dead." Aunt Rachel chuckled. "I'm happy to not be. I don't suppose you can imagine who the person was who waited on him?"

"I can't possibly imagine." Jenn rolled her eyes. "It was like he stumbled upon his own personal detective when he met Doris. That's incredible!"

"You left this part out when you told me your story earlier!" Renee felt a surge of happiness, not unlike she felt when she was told that Jonah had been found.

"I decided to leave some details for the entire audience to enjoy together." Aunt Rachel's expression turned solemn. "While joyful, of course, it opened a wide variety of feelings in my heart. I'm an old woman, my life is almost over. My son is not exactly a young man himself. He's already retired."

"What is his name? I hope we get to meet him." Jenn reached over and squeezed Aunt Rachel's hand.

"His name is Ross Lancaster. He grew up in Washington, D.C., but has lived most of his adult life in Richmond, Virginia. He was married and has two adult children. His wife died of cancer about ten years ago."

"You have grandchildren! How wonderful!" Renee felt the happiness she could see on Aunt Rachel's face.

"After that first visit, he's called me a couple of times for short phone calls. He plans to come visit soon and stay for a few days. I would love for him to meet his cousins."

"Yes, please! We must invite him to your birthday party."

"Slow down, Amber. Aunt Rachel will have to approve that invitation." Jenn looked around the room. "Remember, she's just told us this secret. Besides Doris, I'm assuming that no one in Serendipity knows about Ross' existence. Is that right?"

"Yes. Everyone else who knew I had a child is now dead. I never dreamed that I would be able to introduce my son to my family. I believe that he will be anxious to meet you all. I will have to ask Ross how he feels about coming to my party and being introduced to our friends in the community. At this point in my life, I do not care who knows. I would be proud to introduce him as my son. I can claim no credit though for how wonderful he's turned out."

Aunt Rachel's statement struck Renee in the heart. She could make the same one about Joe. Her little boy had been raised by another woman. She was thankful that Samantha Fairfield appeared to have done a good job. It was still a hard concept for Renee to swallow.

"Thank you for telling us about the loves of your life. These are stories that we did not get to hear while we were growing up. Asking Aunt Rachel questions about her past was frowned upon by your sister, Paisley." Jenn shook her head, affirmatively.

"Paisley was one of my secret keepers, my protectors. It wasn't long after this that she married your father and had the three of you."

"That must have been hard for you to watch." Amber commented.

"It was not hard for me to watch my only sister be happy. That is certainly what your father and the three of you did in her life, you made her happy." Aunt Rachel closed her eyes for a moment. "It was hard to not have that kind of personal happiness for myself. It was all my own doing though. It was my choice not to marry. I had other suitors, before and after Jordan was briefly in my life. None of them invoked the feelings in my heart that Jordan did. Ever how briefly, he was the love of my life."

"The heart loves who the heart loves."

Renee saw the faraway look in Jenn's eyes after she made the statement. Renee had no doubt who Jenn was thinking about, now and in the past.

"Yes. I decided to devote my life to my career. There has not been any shortage of children in my life through all these years. They just did not belong to me. I was able to cherish and nourish them with knowledge. I was able to watch you three grow up to be wonderful women and to love your children as well."

"We are thankful for that, Aunt Rachel." Renee reached over and took her aunt's hand. "We are blessed to be your secret keepers now."

CHAPTER ELEVEN

Jenn

"I don't believe that I've ever in my life been excited about painting." Doris laughed when she returned to the front office after changing clothes. "I had a hard time finding appropriate attire for this activity though."

Jenn could only make brief eye contact with Betsy. She was about to burst into laughter seeing Doris' outfit. A far cry from the woman's normal 1970s Carol Brady polyester, Doris was dressed in a pair of denim bib-overalls with the cuffs turned up several times and a red flannel shirt. She looked like she was ready to be a lumberjack in the woods instead of painting walls in the newspaper office.

"Doris! You look—" Lyle couldn't contain his laughter after abruptly walking into the front lobby. "Darling. You look darling."

"Stop it! I see Jenn and Betsy almost busting a gut trying to hold their laughter inside. I didn't have any clothes that I could stand the thoughts of getting paint on. Do you know how much I pay to dress in my distinctive style? Retro clothing is expensive. So, I went to the thrift store on Ocean Boulevard and found these clothes. It doesn't exactly fit me, but I only paid ten dollars for the outfit."

"Smart and savvy shopper, that's what you are. Betsy and I apologize for our disrespectful giggling."

"Yes, we do. It's just so different from anything I have ever seen you in." Betsy pulled Doris into a hug. "We've worked together for many years. 'Ever' is a long time for us. Personally, I love your 'distinctive style' almost as much as I love the woman who wears it."

"Ladies, it's time to get to painting. Shaun, can you come here and help me?" Lyle yelled into the newsroom.

"Yes, boss, what do you need?"

The lanky sportswriter walked into the front office in the most faded and holey jeans that Jenn thought she'd ever seen. There were already splotches of different colors of paint decorating the jeans and old shirt that the young man was wearing.

"I want you to help me move Doris' desk. Hopefully, we can keep the multiple pieces of the desk together, so we don't have to unscrew all the parts."

"There are some of those sliding disc things underneath already. I had the maintenance man add them years ago so that it was easier for the cleaning crew to move this monstrosity when it was time to clean the carpet."

"That is marvelous. Come on, Shaun, you get on that side."

Jenn and Doris moved out of the way while Betsy went back to her desk. They had closed the newspaper office to the public at noon. Everyone was grabbing a quick slice of pizza after changing their clothes. Jenn had arranged for More Please, a favorite caterer, to bring dinner in that evening after the painting was over. Each department had received detailed instructions from Lyle on how to move desks and other furnishings and equipment away from the walls and to the center of their areas. An order had been placed earlier in the week with Hardy Hardware for all the paint, drop cloths, and other necessary items. Shaun had been sent the day before to pick up the order from his family's store.

A vote had been taken, also by Lyle, to determine the color choices. Jenn opted to leave her office the medium gray that it had been painted before her arrival, less than a year ago. Lyle also wasn't changing his office since he'd used the same color when he rejoined the staff a few months earlier. Besides gray, the other offices would be a medium country blue and a dusty mauve. No one chose white or beige, the dreary standard colors which had adorned the office walls for decades. The thought of every room getting a fresh coat of paint made Jenn smile.

"What are you smiling about, my dear?" Doris whispered from beside Jenn.

"I'm thinking about all the color these walls are going to have in a few hours. The choices are quite soothing and professional looking, but the bottom line is that the walls will have color and I think that's a good thing."

"Me, too. I think it will spark everyone's creativity."

Once Lyle and Shaun had successfully moved Doris' desk to the center of the lobby, Jenn began unfolding a large drop cloth for her and Doris to put over the desk. It would take at least three of them to cover the 'monstrosity,' as Doris called her large desk.

"I heard that you and your sisters had a visit from Rachel earlier in the week. I understand that she shared some information with you three that had been previously withheld."

Jenn noticed the careful way that Doris was choosing her words. The woman had transformed secret keeping into an art form.

"Yes, indeed. The three Halston sisters were shocked and amazed to learn about Richard, Jordan, and Ross." Jenn lowered her voice as she said the names. "We were saddened to learn that we cannot meet the first two but are anxious to have the opportunity to hopefully become acquainted with the third one."

"He's very nice." Doris beamed. "You've seen him though already."

"What? Was I here when he visited the office?" Jenn's eyes bugged out in surprise.

"No, you were not. You saw me with him at Quincy's Diner the day after he met Rachel. You were having lunch with Renee."

"Oh, my goodness! I remember that. I was quite curious about who you were dining with, but I think something later in the day distracted me from asking you about it." Jenn paused, trying to think what it was. "There's been no shortage of distractions in my life since I moved back here."

"Speaking of distractions, I see one peeking through the front door right now."

Jenn turned around to see Randy's nose pressed up again the glass with his hands around his face. They'd put up a large sign to explain why the office was closed, right at Randy's eye level. He had to peek around it to see inside.

'The heart loves who the heart loves,' her own words rang in her head. Jenn certainly knew who her heart loved now. If she was honest with herself, she had loved Randy Nave since she'd known what love was, maybe longer.

Before she could step closer to the door, Doris was already unlocking it.

"Chief Nave, you better have some painting clothes on, if you're coming in here this afternoon." Lyle came around the corner about the time Randy walked through the door.

"The Boss Lady said you all might be able to use an extra set of hands this afternoon. I figured I was due an afternoon off to help the local media." Randy looked in Jenn's direction, winking.

"Can I share that information with my friends at WAVE 104?" Betsy came out of the advertising area with a paintbrush in her hand. "Their offices are in far worse shape than ours are."

"Well, you know, I'd help Gilbert Clock and his team. I can't count the number of times that they've helped us get out a special police alert in a hurry."

Betsy shook her head in understanding.

"You better make sure my painting skills meet Ms. Halston's standards before you farm me out though. I was never that good at staying within the lines when I had to color in school."

"Don't listen to him, Betsy." Jenn rolled her eyes. "I happen to know that Randy learned to paint on one of my father's construction crews when he was still in high school. I remember Dad bragging about Randy's painting skills. That's the reason I mentioned to him what we were doing today."

"Jennifer Halston, I'm shocked! You acted so nonchalant when I offered to come. I guess I'm going to have to watch you." Randy leaned over and whispered in her ear. "I'm going to watch you every chance I get for the rest of my life."

Jenn felt a chill run down her spin. She could hear Doris softly laughing beside her. The woman enjoyed the effect Randy had on Jenn.

"I don't know what you are talking about, Chief Nave." Jenn quickly turned, picking up the final drop cloth that needed to be put on Doris' desk.

"Okay, folks. The show's over." Lyle slapped Randy on the back. "If you're here to work, Chief, I'm going to let you start on that tall wall in the back of Advertising. Everyone on that team seems to be a little vertically challenged."

"What?" Randy furrowed his brow.

"We're all short, Randy." Betsy laughed, heartily.

"Yes, ma'am." Randy saluted Betsy before turning toward Jenn for one last wink.

The afternoon progressed with plenty of painting, a few spills, and lots of laughter. True to what Lyle predicted, it was an experience that built teamwork among the staff and created lots of funny stories for the future. Helen was 'assigned' the story, taking some time throughout the afternoon to take photos of the progress with many 'before and after' shots. It was Lyle's plan to tell the story to readers as part of the invitation to visit the newspaper for the open house that would be held on the day of the Christmas Parade.

When all the offices had been painted, everyone congregated in the back of the building where More Please had laid out several long tables full of their delicious food. As the employees sat around the quiet press that once churned out their newspaper, it brought back memories for Jenn of the first time she'd worked in the building over three decades ago.

"What are you thinking about, Jenn? You look like you're a thousand miles away."

Doris' question brought Jenn back from her memories.

"I wasn't a thousand miles away. I was right here in this room. It was a long time ago though. I was remembering Mr. Charles and Mr. Garland."

"Two of the finest men I've ever known." Doris shook her head.

"I'll agree with that." Helen joined the conversation from a few seats away.

"Mr. Charles' laugh filled the whole building. I could hear him all the way in the front lobby." Doris smiled.

"Mr. Garland was so sarcastic. I was scared of him when I first started working here." Jenn paused, picturing the small man. "He had a wicked sense of humor. Before I left, he became one of my best buddies here."

"Mr. Garland did the layout of every newspaper that was published for over forty years and Mr. Charles ran the press that printed each of those editions." Helen took a deep breath. "Jenn, you probably don't realize this since you weren't living here then. Mr. Charles was working on the press when he had the heart attack that ended his life. He was that dedicated. He hadn't felt well all day but kept it to himself. We finally called an ambulance when we saw him sitting in a chair next to the press, clutching his chest."

Jenn's gaze returned to the big machine that quietly sat in front of them. It didn't seem right that their newspaper was printed in some town in another state and shipped back to Serendipity twice a week. She knew that the press was still in working order. Mr. Sebastian had continued to have it serviced periodically after it stopped being used.

"Do you know if there are any of the former press employees still in the area?"

"Yes. Peter Hernandez worked with Mr. Charles for over ten years. He's the one who took over after Mr. Charles died. Peter lives in Tyrell County. He's a maintenance man for one of the factories over there."

Doris narrowed her eyes, like she was trying to remember something. "I believe that Kaye Vonder is also still somewhere nearby. I haven't seen her in quite a while."

"Kaye lives next door to my cousin over in Wayne County near the Air Force base." Helen spoke up. "Now, there is one memorable woman. She could go toe-to-toe with Mr. Garland on his most persnickety days."

"I think I remember her. She was tall and blonde, with a personality like a force of nature." Jenn pictured the woman in her mind. It had been decades since she'd thought of her.

"That's a pretty good explanation, Jenn. Kaye is a mess. What are you thinking about doing?" Helen asked.

"It seems such a shame that we don't print our own papers. Maybe if we could find some equipment, like the big camera or whatever we made the printing plates on, it would be wonderful to start that press up again."

"You own all that equipment, Jenn." Doris shook her head, affirmatively. "It's in the storage building out back. Don't you remember those items on the inventory list for the building?"

"There were so many things on those sheets and sheets of lists. I probably saw the word 'camera' and thought it was the regular size kind." A big smile began crossing Jenn's face. "If we have all the equipment, all we would need is the supplies, paper, and the people to run it."

"You also have lots of paper, probably enough for a couple of editions. It's in that same building."

"Good grief! What else is in that building? I just glanced in it the day I took possession of the operation."

"There's a museum of stuff out there. Items from every era of this newspaper's one hundred years of operation." Doris wiped a tear from her eye. "You didn't just buy a business, Jenn. You bought a living, breathing member of this community. A lot of local businesses were sad to see the printing of our hometown newspaper go to some big plant far away. It was like a factory moving overseas; it didn't set well with anyone. I think you might find some strong support for a plan to print here again. I also think that at least one of those former press men or women would come back. You've already got one person here who knows how to run that press."

"Who is that?"

"Me."

Jenn turned to find Lyle standing behind her.

"Mr. Sebastian made sure that I learned how to run the press when I was editor the first time. He could operate it as well. You must have two people to run it effectively. Mr. Sebastian was always afraid that something might happen to Mr. Charles. There had to be a backup team."

"That's been quite a few years ago, do you think you would still remember?"

"I wrote a story about it with step-by-step directions. There's also a video of the process, too."

"A video? Can I see it?" Jenn felt a rush of adrenaline. *This is exciting.*

"It's on my YouTube channel." Lyle flashed his famous smile. "You didn't *thoroughly* check *all* my credentials, did you?" Lyle raised his eyebrows, smiling.

That smile. It was dangerous.

"Lyle has quite a popular YouTube channel, Jenn." Helen laughed under her breath. "Guess what the name of it is?"

"I obviously have no idea." Jenn looked from Helen to Lyle to Doris.

"Oh, yes, you do." Doris rolled her eyes.

"It's 'Adventures with Lyle the Smile.'" Lyle winked.

"You're kidding me."

"YouTube is a powerful form of social media and a great way to make side money. I've always known what my nickname was." Lyle shrugged his shoulders. "It's catchy. That's what you need for great social media marketing and popularity. It's mine. I might as well use it. I started my channel about ten years ago. At first, it was short videos about trips I was taking. Then, I decided to expand it to other types of 'adventures,' such as home repairs and cooking. I have one playlist that is all about my work. I revived that old video I made years ago about running the press. I also did videos then about operating that big camera and burning plates for the press as well as how to operate a standard darkroom. I've had hundreds of thousands of views of those videos. People find them interesting."

"That's incredible and a whole other topic of conversation. I'm thrilled to know that you know something about the press. One day, I would love for us to print our newspaper here again. It may take us a while to reach that goal, but I still want to keep it alive."

"If you are that serious about it, let's do some investigative work and find out what it would cost versus what is currently paid to print each edition elsewhere. I'd also like to get some of those former press folks together and see if any of them have interest in returning, even on a part-time basis. Maybe we could start with producing the printed version of the new real estate publication."

"Another incredible idea. Let's keep moving in that direction."

The painting was over. The desks, computers and other furnishings would remain covered until Monday morning when everyone would work together to put their individual department areas back together. Laughter had been abundant and flowing as stories were told around the long table until all were too full of wonderful food.

While the caterers were beginning to clean up from the meal and some of the staff started to leave, Jenn began walking through the building looking for Randy. She'd been so engrossed in her conversation about the press, she didn't notice when he left the room.

Walking from the press area into the advertising offices, Jenn laughed seeing the white 'mountains' of furnishings, large and small. It gave the illusion that she was travelling through a snow village. When she reached the front office, she found the backend of a pair of overalls under the cloths that covered Doris' desk.

"What are you doing under there, Doris?" Jenn lifted the edge of the large white sheet.

"I've lost my shoes."

Jenn laughed at the muffled answer. "Aren't they on your feet?"

"Not those shoes, the ones I had on this morning. I must take them home."

"I'm sure they will be safe under your desk for the weekend." Jenn watched as the woman crawled further under the sheet.

"Finally!" Doris shouted in pleasure before backing her way out, clutching the shoes in her hand. "You may think I'm silly, Jenn, to be so concerned about a pair of shoes." With Jenn's help, Doris stood up.

"I understand your love for your shoes."

"This pair is extra special. I should have known better than to wear them today."

Jenn could almost hear the 'clunk' of the thick wooden heels of the elevated Mary Jane shoes Doris clutched. This pair was vintage, not retro, in brown suede. The wide buckle with a fringed tassel completed the look. Jenn could not say that she paid much attention to Carol Brady's shoes when she faithfully watched the sitcom after school, but she imagined that the actress who made the character of Carol Brady famous thought the shoes were 'groovy.'

"Retro shoes are quite expensive, I'm sure."

"Retro shoes are expensive. These shoes are vintage. They are priceless, Jenn. I'm sure that many think it quite humorous and eccentric that I have modeled my style after a character from a television show from fifty years ago. That doesn't matter to me, it's part of who I am, and I embrace it." Doris bowed her head, looking at the shoes. "These shoes are priceless to me for two reasons. The first reason is because of who they once belonged to. They are original shoes from The Brady Bunch, worn by Florence Henderson."

Jenn's eyes grew large with surprise.

"I'm fortunate that she and I wore the same size."

"My goodness! How in the world did you get them? They must have cost a fortune."

"I'll probably never know who made it possible for me to receive this gift. One day a couple of years ago, I received a package from California. These shoes were inside with a notarized statement of authenticity. There was a short letter explaining what episodes the shoes were worn in. The final sentence said it was a gift from an anonymous person who heard that I was a big fan of Carol Brady's style."

"You never found out anything further?"

"That's the second reason these shoes are so special. They were an anonymous and mysterious gift. I made a phone call to a number I found that was associated with the statement of authenticity, but the person I talked to said she could not reveal who the gift came from."

"I agree. That certainly makes these shoes special. I understand now why you were crawling under your desk. You hold tight to them and go on home. I hope you've enjoyed this afternoon adventure we've had today. I think it was fun."

"Oh, Jenn, it was a wonderful activity. These tired old offices needed a fresh coat of paint. Our team needed to do something fun together." Still clutching her shoes, Doris picked up her tote bag and purse. "We shall all sleep good tonight."

"Have you seen Randy? I came out here looking for him. I hope he didn't get a police call and had to leave."

"I think you will find him in your office." Doris smiled. "Goodnight, Jenn."

"Goodnight, Doris."

Jenn walked to her office. It was quiet. The only light she saw was from a lamp on the side table near her door. Peeking inside, she found Randy sitting on the couch with a little boy sound asleep in his arms. The image warmed her heart. He looked so serene. Randy must have seen her movement because he turned his head in her direction, smiling when their eyes met.

Before Jenn could say anything, she heard Helen whispering behind her.

"It sounds like Randy got Austin to go to sleep."

"Yes, he's out like a light."

"That's my grandson. My daughter dropped him off about an hour ago. I hope you don't mind. She had to go into work early. Jessica is a nurse at the hospital."

"Certainly not. He's adorable."

"Doris fed him a piece of cake. He was wide open, running all over the place for a while. Then, he saw 'Mr. Chief,' as he calls Randy. Austin's father is one of Randy's patrol officers."

"Oh, I didn't know that. They are certainly a family of service to our community."

"Both of them have good hearts and are dedicated to their jobs. Working the hours they do, Austin ends up spending a lot of time with Nana."

Jenn turned to see that Randy had quietly stood up, still holding Austin.

"I'll carry him to your car, Helen. You lead the way."

Jenn stepped back into the lobby so that Randy could walk around her.

"I'll be right back."

Austin snuggled close to Randy's neck. It was a sweet picture. Jenn imagined what Randy might have been like as a young father. For the first time, Jenn's heart yearned for a memory that did not belong to her. The thought caught her off guard, causing tears to fill her eyes.

"Goodnight, Jenn. I enjoyed this afternoon."

Jenn faked a yawn and rubbed her eyes to conceal the emotion from spilling out.

"We had fun, and the offices look wonderful. You have a good weekend, Helen."

Glancing at the front door where Randy was waiting for Helen, Jenn caught him staring at her. His brow was furrowed slightly. She wondered if he'd seen the emotion in her eyes. Quickly, she gave him a big smile. Again, trying to conceal the feelings that had filled her heart.

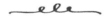

Jenn invited Randy to come back to the beach house so they could take an evening stroll on the beach. The weather was a few degrees warmer than normal. With a light jacket, it was perfect for a walk to burn some of the delicious calories they'd eaten earlier.

Reflecting off the water, the moon provided just enough light to guide their steps. The sound of the waves as darkness approached was soothing, relaxing.

"I think the office looks fabulous." Randy took Jenn's hand in his as they walked. "It's amazing what a little paint can do. That was a cheap remodel."

"I think everyone was tired of those drab whites and beiges that have adorned the walls for decades. I'm happy that Lyle came up with the idea of having a group event. While I know that some of the staff have worked together for many years, I'm not sure how much socializing they've done with each other, especially as a group."

"You have a great staff. I've known several of them for many years. I understand that buying the newspaper was a leap of faith on your part, I don't think you will be sorry with your investment.'

"I'm glad to hear you say that. It was scary to invest so much money on a dream. But the signs kept pointing for me to return to Serendipity and the chance seemed too good to pass up."

"I'm certainly *very* happy that you followed those signs. I'm saddened that one of those signs was the passing of your dear mother. I'm positive that she would be happy you've heeded your instincts to return. Look at all the wonderful things that have happened!"

"Strange, mind-boggling, and miraculous are also words I would use." Jenn took hold of Randy's arm while they continued to walk. "You are on the top of the wonderful list. My brain still can't wrap my mind around being Randy Nave's girlfriend."

"Jenn, you have to realize that you are more than my girlfriend." Randy stopped Jenn, turning her to face him with a hand on each arm.

"You are the love of my life. I knew it when I was a foolish kid. I feel it even stronger as I'm sliding into becoming an old man. Heaven help whoever or whatever tries to stand between me and you spending the rest of our lives together."

"Oh, Randy, I wish—" Before she realized it, tears were streaming down Jenn's face.

"Where are these tears coming from?" Randy gently wiped them away. "I thought I saw some while we were still at the office. What's wrong?"

"Nothing is wrong with today, with life now. I'm just wishing that some parts of life had turned out differently for us."

"Well, I can't say that hasn't been my wish for too many years. But I'm also a firm believer that things happen for a reason and when 'it's time.'" Randy shook his head. "We might have gotten together when we were kids and broken up over something stupid, never having a real chance. This is our chance now. The only person who has the power to discourage me from my dogged pursuit of this chance is you."

"Never! I will not. I cannot. I would have never done to Simon what he did to me. But, once the door was open, I eagerly walked through it. If I'd known you were going to be on the other side of the door, I would have run right into your arms."

Randy pulled Jenn into his strong embrace. She breathed in the 'Randy scent,' feeling his strength, feeling safe.

"What made your tear up at the office?"

"Watching you with Austin, I was thinking what you were like as a young father. For a moment, I was sad that I hadn't been part of that."

"It would have been wonderful, but you and I both have awesome children. We can look forward to being grandparents together. My friends say that's better than raising them yourself." Randy hugged Jenn closer. "We can't go back. We've got to appreciate today and all the tomorrows to come. If we can live what we are preaching to Sinclair, we will take care of ourselves and live to be old folks.'

"In rocking chairs?" Jenn chuckled, wiping her eyes.

"No! I want to be like Mel's parents and keep moving. Old age can't catch up with Mr. and Mrs. Snow because they don't stop long enough. We've got a lot of good years ahead."

"We do. We've also got plenty more working years ahead of us. I can't imagine you retiring; you are so dedicated to your team and the citizens of Serendipity. As far as I'm concerned, does a business owner ever get to retire? I bet my accountant would say no."

"You've got the Oasis to think about as well. I haven't quite wrapped my mind about what you and your sisters are going to do with that. It's an incredible opportunity."

"It's an incredible responsibility. I hope things will fall into place so that we can make it into something that is not only successful but will honor the Bentleys' legacy."

"Excellent vision. The Halston girls will figure it out." Randy rubbed Jenn's forehead. "Quit worrying so much. You know they say that most of the things we spend time worrying about never happen."

"I support that theory. That's why I worry, so those things won't happen." Jenn moved out of Randy's embrace and began twirling around, feeling the breeze on her face, kicking her feet up in the ocean.

"You're amazing!" Randy took hold of her hands, dancing in the surf with her. "I love this life with you."

It's a dream come true.

Chapter Twelve

Amber

"CLAIRE ARRIVES TODAY!"

Amber had to laugh at her sister, Jenn. She and Randy had come in last night with paint in their hair. This morning, Jenn looked like she was going to clean out an attic. Jenn was attired in old clothes with a bandana on her head. It was a comical appearance for her normally professionally dressed older sister.

"Great! What time do you expect her to arrive?" Amber poured her second cup of coffee.

"She texted me about an hour ago saying that she had about two hundred more miles. Since she was driving the moving truck by herself, she split the trip over two days."

Jenn raised her hand as Renee started to speak.

"Don't even ask. I begged her to let Foster come and help her with the driving. She wouldn't hear of it. In fact, Claire said she wasn't even going to tell us when she was leaving to prevent someone from coming. Thankfully, her better judgment won at least on that point. She said she knew it wasn't a good idea for her to be on the road without anyone being aware. She's quite stubborn."

"I can't imagine where Claire got that trait from." Renee stirred a pot of oatmeal.

"I blame Grammie Elana." Jenn raised an eyebrow. "As we've recently learned, those Frederick women are fierce."

"Speaking of our current fiercest one, did you happen to hear from the attorney's office about when we could have access to the Oasis?" Amber accepted the bowl of oatmeal Renee handed to her.

"My goodness, I forgot to tell you two." Jenn walked over to where her purse was sitting on a side table. "Getting back late last evening from the paint party we had at work made me forget."

"And having a romantic stroll in the moonlight with Chief Dreamy." Renee put her hand over her heart, sighing.

"That, too. I talked with Pattie Maxwell yesterday and she told me to stop by and pick up a key." Jenn reached into her purse. She pulled out a key, dangling it in the air. "She also gave us a code for the security system. She mentioned that they have scheduled a housekeeping team to come in each week to check on the house and keep it clean. There was a thorough cleaning done after the police completed their investigation. The items that were determined to be the personal belongings of Mark Blatch were removed and taken into police custody. The housekeeping team also cared for the home when Mr. Bentley was still living, so they had a good idea of what items needed to be taken away and what were personal items belonging to the Bentleys."

"Did Ms. Maxwell happen to mention what day of the week that the housekeeping team comes?"

Renee placed a bowl of oatmeal in front of Jenn and herself. In the middle of the table between all of them, she set a platter of small bowls with a variety of choices of ingredients to add to the hot food including brown sugar, chopped apples, raisins and pecans.

"I'd forgotten how delicious and comforting fresh oatmeal can be." Amber closed her eyes, savoring the warmth and mixture of flavors. *It reminds me of growing up.* Tears formed in her eyes, spilling out when she opened them.

"I know." Renee reached over and squeezed Amber's left hand. "It feels like home. It's also good for you, little sister. Put some extra butter in it. You need the calories."

"Pattie didn't give me those type of details. But she did send me the name and contact information for the company. I think they are the same one that Mom used."

"If that's the case, that company is owned by one of my former classmates, Heather Graham. The company has a cute name, I can't remember it. Mom told me the story behind it. Heather's husband checked out of their relationship early on in their marriage, leaving her with three small children. She had been a stay-at-home mom who kept an immaculate house, so she parlayed those skills into a serious business by creating a cleaning service for Serendipity's ample rental homes. It soon expanded to the neighboring coastal communities. She has a mega business now." Renee paused, eating a bite of her food. "Despite that, she always came with the team who cleaned this house because Mom was one of her first customers."

"Another great success story from our hometown. I hope we've done an article about her business." Jenn scrolled on her phone. "Here is the email, Pattie sent me. Heather's business is called 'You've Got Maids.'"

"Oh, that is clever." Amber smiled. "I've heard you both speak of former classmates who have businesses here or nearby. I wonder if any of my classmates do. I've been in contact with few of them since high school."

"Hopefully, you can connect with some of your old friends while you are staying here." Renee poured each of them more coffee. "Time and distance give you a completely different perspective. I'm finding that I'm forming a totally different connection with those who I've rekindled a friendship with. Our life experiences have a way of tearing down the barriers that perhaps kept us apart when we were younger."

"That's a wonderful explanation, Renee. Some of us had advantages when we were growing up, whether that was in our intelligence or popularity, or even our family's status in the community. Becoming adults and dealing with the myriad of problems that we all face puts us on a more level playing field. It also forces us to see people for who they truly are, good or bad."

"Exactly! Perhaps, Amber, someone will emerge from the past who will be just the type of friend you need at that point in your life. It may even be someone you only casually knew." Renee looked at her buzzing phone. "I'm living proof, in more ways than one, that miracles can happen. I'm reading a text from my son, who is wishing me a good day. I still cannot believe how blessed I am."

Tears poured down Renee's face. Sitting on each side of her, Amber and Jenn reached out to take her hand.

"We are all blessed by each of the miracles we've experienced and the fact that the three of us now get to be together." Jenn squeezed Amber's hand. "Combine that with some of the revelations we are learning about our family, it's a life-changing time."

"Oh, my, yes, Aunt Rachel's revelations alone are shocking and heartbreaking. Let's get back to talking about her party." Amber released both of her sisters' hands, opening a small notebook beside her. "I think we should refresh our memory about the interior of the Oasis before we get too deep into our planning. We need to understand how this party could flow in that space."

"That! That is the exact reason why you are the perfect person to take the lead in operating the Oasis when we inherit it." Renee stood, collecting the empty bowls. "Running a facility like the Oasis comes naturally to you. Your instincts combined with your education and experience will be a winning combination."

"You've got a lot more confidence in my abilities than I do. First things first. Let's take a tour of the property and sketch out some ideas for Aunt Rachel's party. Did I hear one of you mention the idea of making the event a fundraiser for a local charity?"

"Yes. I think that would be dually fitting for Aunt Rachel and the legacy of the Bentleys." Jenn held out her mug for Renee to refill it with coffee. "Aunt Rachel is a legend in education in this area. I'm certain that she would want us to put a 'no presents' notice on the invitation. I'm also certain she would be thrilled to have her birthday benefit a worthy charity. The Bentleys were known for their philanthropy. I think that anything we can do to honor that going forward is an excellent way to thank them for their generosity to us and this community."

"Great! That takes this event to a whole different level. We can make it a black-tie affair with lots of sophisticated glamour." Amber began jotting ideas into her notebook. "Jenn, you also mentioned having a caterer in mind. Was it the same one you used last night for your painting party?"

"Yes, the name of the company is More Please. It was their menus that you dropped off at Aunt Rachel's house the other day. By the way, there was a little food leftover last night, and I had them box it up so that you two could sample some of their delicious flavors. It's in the fridge for you two to snack on later."

"Yum!" Renee rubbed her belly. "I'm planning to go with you to help Claire unload. Amber, don't eat all the goodies while we're gone."

"Michelle assures me that it's not going to take long to unload Claire's moving van. She's enlisted several of their neighbors to help. Knowing Claire, she will want to mostly do her unpacking by herself."

"The apple did not fall far from the tree, Miss Organized." Renee finished loading the dishwasher. "I bet you had a detailed plan for where you were putting each item when you moved in here."

"I wouldn't call it a 'detailed plan.' I might have had a small diagram."

Amber chuckled to herself watching the banter between her two sisters. Because of the closeness in their age, Renee and Jenn always had a bond that Amber did not feel with either of them. Her sisters doted on her and sometimes harassed her, but there wasn't the secret sharing and private jokes. Amber was always a little too young to be included or, in some situations, to understand what her older sisters were doing. She hoped that since they were all three adults now that might change. Maybe the 'sister field' was finally level.

"I'm going to do some research into what type of event rental equipment services are available in the area." Amber continued jotting down notes. "With all of the destination weddings that I'm sure are being held in these coastal towns, I would imagine that there are many different companies that rent tables, chairs, and a wide range of other décor items."

"I believe I have seen advertisements in our newspaper for that very thing. Go to the *Serendipity Sun* website and click on the 'destination weddings' tab. We do a special section on that topic each year, and I believe it has seasonal updates in the online version."

"Excellent! That's exactly where I need to start. That will make my research much quicker." Amber heard a distant buzzing, rising from the table. "I bet that's a text or voicemail from Dawson or Willis. I'm going to take a shower and get dressed. Then I'll call Dawson and Willis. I think I'm going to keep my rental car for another week. Dawson mentioned that I should probably go ahead and buy a vehicle for us to have here, if I can find something I like."

"Maybe Renee or I could take you over to Sinclair's dealership one day this week. We could call him in advance and give him some ideas about the type of vehicle you would like."

"You are referring to Sinclair Lewis, right? He's Mel's boyfriend again." Amber laughed. "I think I might need a cast list to keep up with all these different people. I remember Sinclair. I hope I get to see Mel soon."

"I'd forgotten that you haven't seen her yet. Yes, she and Sinclair are one of those miracles we were talking about earlier. We really shouldn't use the word 'never.' It can end up being a short time."

"I'm glad to hear you did well on the test, Willis. Do you have a lot of homework this weekend?"

After Amber took a luxurious shower in the bathroom off the 'purple bedroom,' as her mother always called it, she heard Jenn and Renee leaving to meet Claire at her new condo.

"I've got a bunch of math homework and a book report to do."

Amber could hear Willis munching on something. She was surprised that he was up so early on a Saturday. The sun was barely up on the West Coast.

"Have you read the book?"

"I've read a few chapters."

"Willis, you better get on that today. Lay off the video games."

"I know, Mom. I've only got about a hundred pages to read. I'll get it done."

The chomping noises continued.

"What are you eating?"

"Cereal. It's my second bowl."

"Anything healthy, dare I ask?"

"The first bowl I had was that crunchy raisin bran stuff. This bowl is corn flakes."

"Well, there are worse breakfasts, I suppose. Where's your father?"

"He left at dawn to meet one of his crews somewhere in the valley. I wanted to go, but he said I had to get this book report done."

"Good answer, Dad!"

"Yeah, I guess. He said we could get pizza and stream a movie tonight, if I got it done."

"That's a lofty goal. You'll have to be focused."

"I really want to see this movie. I've already read a chapter while I've been eating."

"Okay, sweetheart, I will let you go. Text later and update me on your progress. Love you."

"Love you, Mom."

Amber took a deep breath after the call ended. A smile began to cross her face as she thought about how blessed she was. The grip addiction had on her life made Amber feel hopeless for a long time. Now into a strong recovery, she had her beloved son back in her life. Thanks to the devotion of his father, Willis was continuing to grow into a strong young man. She could not believe that Dawson's devotion also extended to her. Amber did not feel like she deserved his love, but given this second chance, she would grab onto it with both hands.

Seeing the notebook laying on the bed, Amber was reminded of the assignment her sisters had given her—planning a spectacular party for their beloved aunt. Since the three of them were on the verge of inheriting the Oasis from Walter Bentley, Amber knew that she was also auditioning to possibly oversee the operation of the fabulous property. She did not have enough faith in herself yet to believe she could rise to such a goal. Maybe working on this special party would help build her confidence.

Amber chose the small table in the kitchen to begin the research. Opening the laptop Jenn left her to use, Amber first went to the newspaper's website to find the special section about destination weddings. Jenn was correct, the section had an exhaustive list of local and regional vendors who specialized in providing services to those who sought to have their special day in the coastal town of Serendipity or nearby. Amber was impressed to see the level of amenities that could be utilized in their small hometown. After using the section to locate several vendors she thought might be needed, Amber began to email some of them to inquire their availability for New Year's Eve. That would be the tough part, especially since the event was now less than two months away.

Two hours and a whole pot of coffee later, Amber had found multiple potential vendors for every type of equipment, furnishing, and decorative need she envisioned for that night. Having emailed each one of the vendors as she found them, Amber was amazed that a couple of them had already responded to her with availability and further information or respectful messages saying they were booked. Two of those who had declined even offered a suggestion of another vendor in the area. Amber was impressed that there was such a network of businesses that they felt comfortable and confident about recommending their competitors. She was about to send one of them a message asking further questions when she heard a female voice coming through the kitchen window. Turning around, she saw the familiar face of Gladys Fox, the delightful woman who lived next door.

"Gladys! It's wonderful to see you." Amber opened the sliding glass door, pulling the neighbor into a hug.

"My darling girl, you are the one it's wonderful to see!" Gladys held Amber at arm's length, before pulling her back into a strong hug.

Amber breathed in the scent of the long-time Halston family friend. Gladys always smelled like lavender and exotic tea. She had forgotten that an embrace from Gladys was like a relaxing tonic.

Opening the door for Gladys to go inside, Amber took in the woman's colorful outfit. Wearing one of her signature kaftans, the multicolor long dress reminded Amber of a piece of stained glass artwork with the fabric pattern being bright geometric shapes on a solid black background. Bright red clogs completed the look. As Gladys walked in front of her, Amber saw a large straw hat was hanging down her back. The woman was dressed for beach walking.

"I came over to see if one of the Halston sisters might want to take a walk with me. I didn't realize that you had returned from California. I'm so happy to see you."

"I'd love to go for a walk with you, Gladys. Sit down for a moment while I go put on my tennis shoes and get a light jacket."

"We've got a lot of catching up to do, young lady. I want to hear all about what it's like in rehab."

Gladys continued to talk while Amber walked to her bedroom. It surprised her a little that the woman wanted to hear about her treatment. Most people tried to avoid the topic. She should have remembered that most people weren't Gladys Fox. Amber quickly found her shoes and jacket. Gladys kept loudly talking from the kitchen.

"And that yummy husband of yours. I want to know what he's been up to. I know, he's not your husband at the moment, but I hear he's going to be again. Don't waste too much time retying that knot, young lady. Dawson is a keeper. Even your mother thought so."

"She did?" Amber came up behind Gladys.

"Paisley thought that Dawson was a fine man. He was quite respectful. He kept your mother thoroughly informed when you were in rehab the first time. Dawson took the blame for what was happening. He said you became addicted because of the people you met in his celebrity life."

"It's not his fault. I'm an adult. I made my own decisions."

"Paisley realized that. She did appreciate his efforts to protect you in her eyes." Gladys stood up. "Let's get walking. The temperature is supposed to start dropping in an hour or so. I walk to feel the sun on my face while I can. Where's Jenn and Renee?"

"Claire is arriving today. They are helping her move into the condo she's renting from Foster and Michelle." Amber closed the door, following Gladys across the deck and down the steps to the beach.

"Wonderful! We aren't too far from having the entire family in Serendipity. I did hear correctly that you are planning to make a home here as well?"

"That's what Dawson and I have been discussing. I'm really surprised that both he and Willis are anxious to move here. I would have thought that Dawson wouldn't want to leave the business he's worked so hard to build in someone else's hands. I'm also surprised that Willis is willing to leave his friends in California."

"Did the three of you live in a coastal community in California?"

Gladys carefully maneuvered through the uneven patches of sand, occasionally grabbing Amber's arm as they walked toward the ocean.

"No, we were about an hour away from the Pacific Ocean."

"Bingo! Maybe Willis wants to learn to surf."

"That could be." Amber laughed, picturing her lanky son on a surfboard. "I wish there was someone in the family who could teach him."

"Maybe Foster still remembers how or maybe my nephew could teach him."

"Your nephew?" Amber tried to remember if anyone had mentioned Gladys having a nephew in Serendipity.

"Yes, Wade. Wade Stanley. Stanley was my maiden name. He's my youngest brother's son. Age wise, Wade should probably be my great-nephew. It was almost like my brother and his wife had a second family."

"Oh, is he the young man who used to come spend some summers with you? I think I might have met him once on a trip home to visit my folks."

"Yes, Wade spent two summers here. The timing of Claire returning to Serendipity is certainly a happy accident. Claire and Wade had a little romance the second summer he spent here."

"I don't remember hearing about that. I guess I was too caught up in my own life then."

Amber and Gladys walked just above where the tide would roll in to keep their feet out of the water. Looking up, Amber was surprised to see the bright sun against a blue sky. It was an unseasonably warm fall day. The forecast did predict storms to roll in after sunset.

"As you should have been, I would say that you were deep into your own new life by then. I cannot remember what year it was. Wade was the only one in his family to ever come and spend a summer with me. It was a long trip from Boston. I don't think his siblings wanted to be away from their friends that long to stay with a stuffy old aunt."

"Goodness! I don't think the word 'stuffy' has even been used to describe you, Gladys. There was a time or two I got into trouble for spending too much time at your house when I was growing up, because I was supposed to be visiting my grandparents. Now, you could use the word 'stuffy' to describe them at times."

"My dear, Carson and Elana were from another time. It's been an interesting ride to know so many generations of your family. My house was the first one that was built after your grandparents built theirs. Your father oversaw the construction. Once he and your mother retired next door, Marshall was continually coming over and tinkering with things that needed fixing. I think he liked my house better than his own, probably because my husband and I basically let him design it."

"You do have a beautiful house. I don't remember Dad building it."

"That's because you weren't born yet. Renee and Jenn were both still toddlers. I remember visiting the construction site one day and your mother stopped by. She had the girls with her. Renee and Jenn played in the sandpile that had been brought in for the concrete. They made some sort of dune or fort in it and climbed in. Your mother had a time finding them."

"I bet that didn't end well for my sisters." Amber giggled.

"Nope. I imagined that neither one of them hid from their mother again."

Amber looked up at the Oasis as they approached it. Her mind went in a dozen different directions, thinking about all the events that could be hosted in the grand home.

"All these years I have been a neighbor to this beautiful house, I've always wondered what would happen to it when the Bentleys were gone."

Gladys interrupted Amber's thoughts. "I'm certainly glad that imposter was outed before something horrible happened to the Oasis. I have a feeling that Walter had a plan for if there wasn't a descendant to inherit it. Walter was brilliant. He knew that the candidates in his family tree were few. I bet he planned for that."

"I bet you're right." Amber smiled to herself. She knew that Gladys would be one of the first people her sisters would want to tell when the transfer of the Oasis became official. The lawyers had assured Jenn that the announcement could be made to the public by the time of Aunt Rachel's party. They would certainly reveal the truth to Gladys long before that.

"Let's walk all the way down to the pier and back." Gladys pointed in front of them. "That will give you plenty of time to tell me all about what it's like to be in rehab. I'm interested to know about the phases of your treatment."

For the next hour, Amber described to Gladys what it was like to be a patient in rehab while they made the long walk to the pier and back. She also related how the facility she'd recently been in differed from the first one she experienced several years ago. Gladys asked good questions, only interrupting Amber's story when she didn't understand something. It was cathartic to Amber to talk about it from a treatment point of view, not dwelling on the behavior that forced her to have to go there.

That's what conversations with Gladys had always been for Amber. Even as a teenager, Amber had enjoyed talking to her grandparents' eccentric neighbor. Gladys listened more than she talked when someone was pouring their heart out to her. She always had a funny story to make you forget your troubles. The woman saw the world through her own lens. Gladys' viewpoint was like her fashion statement, bright and unusual, too much for some, but always entertaining.

"My puppies are tired." Gladys pointed to her feet when they reached the steps to climb back to the houses. "That's what happens when you spend too much time lounging on cruise ships. Maybe you and I can catch a few more walks before the winter breeze makes us wish we lived even further south."

"I'd love it. There's nothing like a walk on the beach to clear your head."

Amber followed Gladys up the steps. She tried to mentally figure out how old the woman was. They'd just walked for over an hour on the beach, yet the woman climbed the steps in record time.

"I enjoyed hearing about your adventures in rehab." Gladys rested for a moment after they reached the driveway that separated their two properties. "I had a sister who spent time in rehab several decades ago. I don't think they were as progressive as the facility you were in. Maude never overcame her addiction to alcohol. The complications from it eventually took her life."

"I'm sorry to hear that, Gladys. I didn't know."

"It was a long time ago. She never came to visit. It looks like your sisters have returned. I'm anxious for Claire and Wade to meet again on the sand." Gladys winked. "He's staying with me until he can find a place of his own. Maybe he'll buy one of those condos, too. Thanks for the walk, my dear."

A few minutes later, after spraying off her shoes, Amber walked into the kitchen, finding Jenn staring into the refrigerator and Renee nowhere in sight.

"How did move-in day go?"

"Hey, Amber, it went fine. I now have two children living in my same zip code again." Jenn closed the fridge door. "Claire did some incredible downsizing before she moved. Apparently, Derek was keen to keep a lot of the household items they had. A few of the items had come from his family anyway when they got married, like an antique set of dishes. He bought her out of some of the kitchen stuff and kept most of the furniture. She'll have to go shopping for some items. She doesn't have a toaster or a can opener."

"At least she didn't have to pack that stuff. I didn't expect you two to be back this early. I took a walk on the beach with Gladys."

"I bet you enjoyed that. Gladys has been anxious to see you. We expected to have a longer day, but Claire didn't have as many boxes as I thought she would. Foster and Joe already had the few pieces of furniture she brought off the truck when we arrived. Megan was there, too; she helped Michelle bring in boxes while Renee and I unpacked them and Claire organized. She's basically completely unpacked except for some of her clothes and about ten boxes of books, art, and files for her office."

"We're pooped, at least I am." Renee came around the corner. "I'd forgotten that I've recently taken more than my fair share of chemotherapy. My body wasn't quite ready for lifting things. I've got to get back in shape. In other news, I'm hungry."

Amber laughed at the funny face Renee made. It reminded her of the crazy looks her sister would give her over their mother's shoulder. Renee could go from crazy face to a serious, concerned look in less than two seconds.

"I got so caught up with doing research for Aunt Rachel's party, I didn't even think about starting anything for dinner." Amber looked at the laptop and notes she'd left strewn across the kitchen table. "Why don't we order some takeout?"

"What was the name of that Mexican restaurant that used to be on Main Street?" Renee squinted, like she was trying to remember.

"It had a simple name years ago—The Mexican Restaurant." Jenn smiled. "It's still owned by the same family. The food is even better than you remember. It's called La Siesta now. I think I have one of their menus in the junk drawer."

Amber watched Renee dig around the drawer, finally pulling out a multicolored brochure with a sombrero on the front. Each of them took turns reading over the menu before making selections and calling in an order. About an hour later, a young man showed up at the door with their food.

"There are some good Mexican restaurants in California where we live, but I'm not sure I've ever had a better tortilla soup than this one." Amber took another spoonful of the delicious dish. "This could be addictive, and I don't kid around about that."

"I know. I order that soup and use it as an excuse to eat lunch at my desk." Jenn took a bite of her burrito. "That way I can slurp up all of those wonderful ingredients in the privacy of my own little world."

"What all is in it?" Renee dug her fork deep into her order of nachos.

"I believe it is a chicken stock with a wonderful assortment of herbs and spices, but it also includes rice, tomatoes, onions, huge chunks of shredded chicken, avocado with queso cheese and tortilla chips on top." Jenn rattled off the ingredients like she was reading a menu.

"You certainly know that well." Amber laughed, savoring the flavors. "There seems like there's something else in it."

"It's got to be some secret magical ingredient." Jenn laughed. "I really don't care. It's heaven in a bowl."

"Can I stick my spoon in there, little sister?" Renee precariously waved her spoon close to Amber's bowl.

"Are you asking me to share, big sister? Hmmm, let me think about the times in our childhood when I asked you to share with me." Amber giggled, enjoying the moment, before sliding the bowl toward Renee. "Make sure you get a little bit of everything to make the tasting complete."

Doing as Amber instructed, Renee had a rather large serving on her spoon. She rolled her eyes when her tasting was complete.

"Jenn, we'll be asking you to bring each of us one of those soon. Yum. All this food is fabulous."

"Yes. Randy took me for my first visit. We had a little bit of a disagreement on that lunch date."

"You did not fight with the most wonderful man in Serendipity." Renee scowled.

"Don't worry. It was short-lived. That was the same day that he kissed me on Main Street."

"What!?" Amber spewed soup, almost choking.

"Little sister, our Jenn has had some scandalous behavior in the Downtown District with Serendipity's Police Chief. I have a photo of it."

Renee got up from the table, returning with her phone. After scrolling for a few seconds, Renee turned the phone to face Amber.

"Oh, my goodness! I realize that you have been seeing Randy. I was not prepared to see a photo of you two locking lips like teenagers. This was out in public?"

"It was right in front of the newspaper office. I would say that our sister should be ashamed of herself, if I didn't think it was the most wonderful thing in the world." Renee waved her hands in celebration. "Guess who sent me the photo?"

"I couldn't even begin to guess." Amber glanced at Jenn. Her sister was nonchalantly eating her meal.

"It was Aunt Rachel. The sister of our mother knew about Jenn making kissy face with Randy before I did."

"Aunt Rachel has an informant." Jenn spoke between chews. "Doris is like an operative with the CIA or something. She's stealth."

"I've got to say that I think it's fabulous that you are dating Randy. I adored him when I was a child. He was so sweet and handsome. I always knew that he was in love with Jenn. Didn't you, Renee?"

"Everyone within a ten-mile radius of Randy and Jenn knew that Randy was in love with Jenn, except for Jenn, and probably Randy."

"I'm not even going to fight this teasing any longer. I'm head-over-heels for Randy Nave and I don't care who knows it. I even told Simon in so many words when he showed up here unannounced a couple of weeks ago."

"What?!" Amber spewed soup again. "I love this soup. Please stop saying things that make me waste it."

Jenn and Renee howled in laughter.

"Simon? Your ex-husband, Simon, came to visit? Please don't tell me that he's moving here, too. Now that you are divorced, I have a confession. I never really liked Simon." Amber gave Jenn an apologetic look.

"It's okay, Amber. It would appear that's a common opinion in this family. He's not one of my favorites anymore either." Jenn took a drink of her beverage. "Simon was thinking about moving here, but I believe Foster has dissuaded him from that idea."

"Jenn, you're not telling the story correctly. Randy was really the one who dissuaded Simon. Randy's very presence made Simon rethink his plans."

Amber listened intently while Jenn and Renee recounted the details of Simon's new life including his impending child. She laughed aloud when Jenn told the part about Randy calling Foster in front of Simon.

"Randy is wonderful on many levels, isn't he?"

"He is." Jenn tilted her head, sighing and smiling.

"It's only a matter of time, Amber, before Randy is our brother-in-law. Neil is so excited." Renee shook her head, raising her eyebrows. "Dawson will love him, too. Remember, Randy was a big athlete in high school."

"Dawson loves the idea of being here with all of you. He came from a close family, but most of them are deceased now. He was the youngest. He's anxious for Willis to grow up around family."

"I wish he had some cousins closer to his own age." Renee reached over and squeezed Amber's hand. "Jenn and I had our children early. With you being several years younger than us, it's made a gap."

"Willis will make some great friends here in no time. Growing up in a small town makes friends seem like family." Jenn finished the last of her meal. "Speaking of family, how did your researching go for Aunt Rachel's party?"

"Fabulous! The *Serendipity Sun* does indeed have a great section on planning a destination wedding. I would suggest that you expand that in the future to include reunions. That was a big niche I cultivated at the resort I worked at in California. There are a variety of different types besides family ones, there's also all branches of the military, sororities and fraternities, and many others."

"What a great idea! I bet that Mel already works with reunions through the Visitors Bureau."

"She probably does. These coastal towns would make great reunion locations." Amber turned around, picking up her notepad from the counter behind her. She briefly scanned the list she'd made. "I was amazed that several of the local and regional vendors I contacted responded to me on a Saturday. They really have their fingers on the pulse of the market. I was a little concerned about the party being held on New

Year's Eve. I was pleased to find that there were still several vendors who had availability and were willing to take on an event that night. I believe I've located most of our key needs, except for a band or a DJ."

"That would definitely be a category where I think Mel could help."

"Good. What do you think about us going over to the Oasis tomorrow and taking a look around? Do you feel comfortable doing that?" Amber looked from Jenn to Renee. Both looked a little apprehensive.

"Is it me or does that feel wrong?" Renee was the first to speak. "I feel like we are kids planning to sneak into some building we don't belong in."

"It's our mother's voice we hear in our head. 'Never go inside someone's home unless they invite you.'"

"Oh, that hurt, Jenn. I could almost hear Mom when you said that." Amber's eyes filled with tears.

"Me, too." Renee scooted her chair closer to Amber, pulling her into a hug.

"Why don't I see if I can reach Pattie Maxwell?"

"She's the attorney in charge, right? Do you think she'd want to come out on a Sunday?" Amber dried her eyes.

"She seems very nice. Maybe she would enjoy an afternoon lunch at the beach." Jenn began flipping through her phone. "I think she gave me her cell number."

"This isn't exactly the best season for beach visits."

"I checked the forecast earlier. Tomorrow is supposed to be relatively warm. Claire mentioned that she'd like to come over and take a walk on the beach. Since it's a Sunday, I'm hoping she might run into Wade."

"Gladys mentioned him on our walk today. It's crazy how many people who have connections to each other are returning to Serendipity all at once."

"We can call it happy accidents or wonderful second chances. Either way, it's opening doors for people I love to revisit joy for their lives. I'm thrilled."

Amber watched Jenn beam with happiness. She'd seen the same type of expression on Renee's face several times. *I've never seen my sisters happier. I want some of that.*

"Why don't you try to contact Pattie and invite her to come over for brunch and then take us inside for a visit into the Oasis?" Renee spoke while picking up their dishes.

"If we could tour the house tomorrow, it would give me an idea of how we might be able to use the layout in the planning of the event. Most of the events we used to go to over there were beach or pool parties."

"We did attend some Christmas parties over there." Renee began loading the dishwasher. "That was a long time ago though. There could be aspects of the house which have changed since then."

"I texted Pattie. She immediately responded saying that she'd be happy to come for brunch. From what I gathered from a previous conversation, she was involved in checking the inventory of the house after Mark Blatch was arrested, so I think she should be able to give a good tour."

"I better get to planning a menu. I might need to run out to the grocery store."

"You two have already worked so hard today. I hate for you to have to go back out."

"It's okay. Entertaining energizes me. Brunch is relatively easy, if you plan it right. I need to take a quick shower. I'll come up with a menu while I'm doing that. Amber, will you finish loading the dishwasher?"

"Sure. I'll clean up the kitchen. This party is really taking shape. One of the next items on the list should be getting Aunt Rachel to decide on which charity we will have this fundraiser to benefit."

"Let's make plans for the three of us to go see her this week. We haven't shared the news about this inheritance with her." Jenn picked up her phone. "Pattie just texted that she has some news to share about the process, too. Maybe we are getting closer to a resolution. If you don't mind cleaning up the kitchen by yourself, I'm going to go take a shower, too. Then, I can go shopping with Renee."

While Amber worked on loading the dishwasher and straightening up the kitchen, her mind wandered to all the aspects of her life that had changed in a couple of short weeks. A feeling of bliss and contentment began filling her heart. Being reunited with her son and the love of her life was only the beginning. Having her two strong sisters surrounding her with encouragement and support was a special elixir for her soul. Reawakening her passion for work was exciting her in ways she never thought she'd experience again. *This is what healing feels like.*

CHAPTER THIRTEEN

Jenn

"PATTIE, THANK YOU SO much for taking time out of your weekend to give us a tour."

Jenn stood on the sidewalk at the front door of the Oasis with her two sisters and Pattie Maxwell. A feeling of anticipation coursed through Jenn's veins. It had been many years since Jenn had been inside the impressive mansion. To think about walking into the grand home as its owner was more than her heart could stand.

"After that delicious meal and entertaining conversation, I'm the one who should be thanking you. How do I get a regular spot on your Sunday brunch list?"

Today was the first time that Jenn had met Pattie face-to-face. During their numerous email exchanges and brief phone calls, Jenn's mental image of the woman's appearance was something akin to a prosecutor on a television show like *Law & Order*. On this fall weekend day, Pattie was not dressed in a dark business suit with perfect hair and makeup, the middle-aged person who stood at the door with a key in her hand wore jeans with a layered sweater set and her gorgeous dark hair pulled up in a loose ponytail. Her light makeup gave a fresh, natural look that did not completely hide the lines which time had bestowed on her. Jenn felt an instant connection with the woman. She could envision them becoming friends.

"Consider yourself on the list!" Renee answered with fervor. "You, my new friend, hold the keys to the kingdom in your hand. We peasants are going to need all the help we can get on this crazy new journey we are embarking on."

"I admit that taking over this property is not for the faint of heart. I sense a great deal of strength and smarts in the three of you though. Walter Bentley would not have left his beloved home to you if he did not think the 'Halston girls' could handle it."

Pattie turned back toward the door, slipping the key in the lock. Jenn heard the snap of the first, then the second deadbolt. A home as grand as the Oasis needed secure locks. It was ironic to think that the most untrustworthy person to ever pass over the threshold was invited in as a welcomed guest—accepted as a member of the Bentley family. Jenn was thankful that she'd played a small role in revealing Mark Blatch's real identity. That revelation was a miraculous blessing for everyone.

The door opened and the grandeur of the mansion could be seen in every direction. Before even taking a step inside, Jenn could see the light spilling into the room way off in the distance from the floor-to-ceiling windows that served as the wall on the ocean side. All four floors took full advantage of the incredible ocean views on that side of the house.

"It's everything that I remembered it to be." Amber scooted past Jenn, walking across the slate-colored tile floor. "It was so enchanting to visit here. Yet, I always felt at home. Would you agree, my sisters?"

"Yes, that is how I remember our visits." Renee walked through the spacious foyer, stopping occasionally to look down one of the many hallways leading to the first floor wings. "I used to often stay with our grandmother and was sent over here to bring or retrieve something. Mrs. Bentley and our Grammie Elana were like sisters."

"Remind me what Mrs. Bentley's first name was." Pattie followed Jenn as all of them walked deeper into the home.

"Zella." Jenn responded to Pattie's question. "Like our Grammie, Zella Bentley had a strength of character that set her apart. The story goes that Walter Bentley bought acres and acres of this land as a business investment. He planned to partner with our grandfather to build luxurious beach houses and sell them. That all changed one Sunday afternoon when he brought his wife along to see the property. Zella wanted her home to be here, and she wanted their best friends, our grandparents, to be their closest neighbors."

"I did not know that part of the story. I presume that Walter was already building his fortune by then." Pattie sat down on the couch that faced the wall of windows.

"Yes, it was the early 1970s by then. Our grandfather, Carson Frederick, had been constructing buildings for Walter for several decades by that point. They'd both built strong businesses, although Walter's was more lucrative financially."

"Miss Zella, as we called her, fell in love with this property. The Bentleys and our grandparents had nice homes in other parts of Serendipity." Renee spoke from the side front room that was off the main living room. "Our Aunt Rachel still lives in the Frederick family home. Miss Zella insisted that this house and the one next door be built as soon as possible so that the Bentleys and Fredericks could finally be neighbors. Both properties were built in stages with remodeling and additions occurring several times through the years."

"So, the Oasis was not always this grand?" Pattie rose from the couch, following Jenn into the expansive kitchen that was on the left side of the house. "I love this kitchen. It looks like it should be the set for a modern-day Julia Child cooking show."

"The Oasis has always been grand." Jenn hesitated before opening one of the mahogany kitchen cabinets. "It grew in grandeur as the decades passed. Do you know what will happen to the furnishings and other belongings in the home?"

"We had to supervise the inventorying of the house. Some of the art is designated to be sent to museums and galleries, per the Bentleys' request. The personal items, such as clothing, are to be donated to various charities. The rest of the furnishings are to stay with the home, including the contents of this and the other kitchens."

"I forgot there was more than one kitchen in this house."

Jenn left Pattie on the main level. Like her sisters, she began to wander around the stately house alone. Amazingly, throughout the next thirty minutes investigating each room, she never crossed paths with either of her sisters—the house was that spacious.

She wasn't sure that she'd ever been through the entire house before. It pleased her to see that there were ten bedrooms were spread out over multiple floors. Some had personal bathrooms. She couldn't help but wonder if Zella and Walter had not planned the design of the home with the idea that one day it might be a resort. Each floor seemed to have a theme to its look and décor. Each room was a different main color with furnishings that matched perfectly. Jenn's mind began to brainstorm names for each suite, and she recorded notes into her phone to capture what she was seeing and the ideas that flowed.

When their individual tours ended, the three sisters rejoined Pattie in the living room.

"Did you enjoy your tours?"

Pattie's question caused all three of them to begin talking at once. Each of them giving animated details regarding aspects of the house that personally caught their attention. When their descriptions were over. Pattie raised her hand, laughing under her breath.

"I'll take that as a 'yes.' Now, I have another question. The Bentleys only had one son. Do you know why they built such a large home?"

Jenn looked at Renee. There was something about the question that jarred a memory in her, but she couldn't quite conjure the conversation.

"Maybe Aunt Rachel could give a clearer answer to that." Renee was first to speak. "I have this vague memory of hearing our father say that Zella wanted a bedroom for every child she didn't get to have."

"That's it! I was trying to remember what was said." Jenn shook her head affirmatively. "I remember Mom's sad expression."

"Something happened to Miss Zella when she gave birth to Jearl. I believe she had to have a hysterectomy. They were such loving people, I'm not sure why they didn't adopt." Renee narrowed her eyes, like she was searching for a memory in her mind. "It wasn't a topic that was discussed often with our young ears around."

"That's understandable. It is certainly none of my business. Just a question of curiosity." Pattie rose from the chair she was sitting in. "Do you think the layout of the house will work for the event you were discussing this morning? I'm anxious to meet this 'Aunt Rachel' you talked about. She sounds like an interesting woman."

"Aunt Rachel is a force of nature." Jenn smiled broadly, thinking of her aunt. "She's quite well known in this community through her years in education and involvement with many different organizations and charities. I think her beloved status combined with the voracious curiosity that people have about the Oasis will make this an extremely successful event."

"The key will be for us to pair great entertainment and food with a perfect charity and offer it at a price that will not defeat the purpose." Amber's eyes darted back and forth, like she was picturing it all in her mind. "The ticket will be pricey, but our goal will be that the experience will make attendees take out their checkbooks and make contributions directly to the worthy cause. This could become the signature yearly event for the Oasis."

"You all sound like you've already been thinking about what you might want to do with the property. Care to share any of that with your new lawyer friend?" Pattie winked.

"We've not made any real plans." Jenn looked at Renee and Amber. "As you can probably tell, Amber has a background in hospitality and event planning. She worked for several years for a high-end resort in California."

"I've been out of the field since before my son was born and he's a teenager now."

"Don't discount yourself, Sis." Renee chimed in. "It may have been a few years ago, but Amber has a portfolio full of planning events for some high-profile celebrities and businesspeople. Jenn and I think she could turn the Oasis into an elegant resort property. We need to do more research though into what works on the East Coast."

"No doubt this is a mansion that rivals some you may have seen in California." Pattie continued to walk around. "I've heard some of the history about your grandfather building the original part of the house. Was it your father who did the additions and remodels?"

"Yes, our father, Marshal Halston, and Renee's husband, Neil Davenport."

"Davenport. That's ironic. On Friday, I got a speeding ticket. The officer's name was Davenport. I don't imagine it could be any relation."

"Well, was he tall, young, and handsome? With maybe the initials J.H.?" Renee asked as she squinted her eyes.

"Yes, he was all those things. I'm not sure about the initials."

"Was he with the Serendipity Police Department?"

"Yes. I was trying to get to the courthouse for a case. I was speeding. I was also extremely late after getting stopped for it."

"I think you might have met Renee's son, Joe. He recently joined the PD. Sorry about that." Jenn smiled.

"It was my fault no doubt. He was polite and courteous. I've got to admit that he seemed a little familiar, but I don't suppose he could be, if he's only recently joined the PD."

"We could keep you in suspense and make excuses, but since it was international news, there doesn't seem to be any point in doing that." Renee nodded at her sisters. "Joe was kidnapped twenty years ago and was recently found by Police Chief Randy Nave after my incredibly wonderful part-time detective sister recognized that grown-up Joe looks almost identical to his father at that age."

"That's incredible!" Pattie's eyes bugged out in surprise. "I knew that I had seen that handsome face before. When I first heard that report, I burst into tears; I was so happy that he was found. It's every mother's worse fear. I remember when he was taken all those years ago. What a strong woman you must be, Renee."

"Our sister has the fortitude and strength of a Greek goddess." Amber beamed. "Remember them from school? They were also depicted as beautiful statues carved in granite."

"After all these years, they also have chips in them, sometimes a whole arm is missing. That's the way the chemo made me feel."

"Chemo?" Pattie looked from Renee to Jenn.

"Our strong sister also won a battle with cancer." Jenn pulled Renee into a side embrace. "It was the power of love that cured her. Literally. The doctor said so."

"I'm so happy for you, for your entire family." Pattie put her hand over her heart. "I feel honored to have the opportunity to work with and get to know all of you."

"We appreciate your help so far. We've just started on this new adventure with the Oasis." Jenn took a deep breath. "Do you have any idea how much longer it will be before this situation is settled?"

"It probably will not be official before the holidays, but I would expect the process to be complete by early next year. Everything that is happening now, from a legal standpoint, are formalities. The courts in both of Parker Bentley's residences in Europe have confirmed that he is indeed deceased and had no legal heirs. The clause in Walter Bentley's will that allowed for you three to inherit the Oasis is ironclad without legal heirs. But, because of this situation having an international connection *and* the criminal issues with Mark Blatch, it will take time for all the documents to go through the proper channels."

"We aren't sure if that makes us relieved or terrified." Amber laughed. "I'm still getting used to this idea. I only recently learned about the Bentleys' wishes for us to inherit this beautiful home. My sisters have had a little longer to get used to the idea."

"I believe that Mr. Wolff, Walter Bentley's personal attorney, will also want to share some details that only he knows about Mr. Bentley's wishes."

"That would be wonderful!" Jenn reached for her buzzing phone. It was a text from Foster. "We are not sure about this, but we think that our Aunt Rachel may have kept company with Mr. Wolff in the past. It would be delightful to see them reunited on the dance floor during her party."

"Mr. Wolff reminds me of one of those classic actors from the Golden Days of Hollywood. Someone like Jimmy Stewart or Cary Grant. He's not quite *that* handsome, but he has that kind of charisma." Pattie raised her eyebrows as she spoke.

"We've got to meet this man before the party." Renee nodded. "I feel a little matchmaking coming on. Pattie, our aunt never married. We've only recently learned that at least two loves of her life ended in sad and tragic ways. The thought of giving her not only a night of celebration, but maybe also a sprinkle of romance is more than my Hallmark Channel loving heart can stand."

"We can make that happen. Mr. Wolff will want to be front and center for anything that even remotely has to do with the Bentleys. He also remembers your family fondly. There may not have been anyone happier to hear the real story of Mark Blatch than Mr. Wolff. He despised the man when he was impersonating Parker Bentley. He couldn't believe that the man was Walter Bentley's grandson. Now we know that his instincts were correct."

"This is going to be an exciting experience from beginning to end." Amber smiled broadly at her sisters. "If we can make this a night for Aunt Rachel to remember, I think we will also have a great foundation for making the Oasis a place for the public to love."

"I'm so glad I was able to catch you to have lunch today. I feel like it's been forever since we talked."

Jenn had some takeout delivered to her office so that she and Mel could have a private lunch. She needed to enlist her best friend's help with the party for Aunt Rachel, but first she had to tell Mel why they would be allowed to use the elegant property.

"I'm so sorry that I've been a neglectful friend. I've had so much going on lately with work and Sinclair."

"How is he doing?"

"Marvelous. He's walking every morning and going to work out with Randy three times a week. I think he's mostly been sticking to his diet. He's already dropped twelve pounds. It's crazy. I'm doing a lot of the same things and I've barely lost two."

"Men's metabolisms are so much nicer to them than ours are. You keep going. I remember reading an article that said you are more likely to keep weight off when you lose it slowly. Losing one pound a week would equal fifty in a year."

"I know. I don't have that much patience." Mel sighed, taking a drink from her big water bottle. "What's been going on in your world?"

"I feel like I'm always going in twelve different directions. Claire arrived on Saturday, and we helped get her moved into her condo and mostly unpacked. The poor child was diagnosed with both ear and sinus infections before she left Atlanta. It's got to be all that international travel she's been doing. She was hyped up on antibiotics and steroids when she arrived. I think she slept the next two days. I've not bothered her. I know that Michelle and Foster are nearby and have been taking her some food. Randy has been teaching a class at the regional police academy, so that's made some long days for him. Renee and I have been spending as much time as possible with Amber. We've also given her a project to work on. That's one of the reasons I wanted to talk to you today. We've put her in charge of planning Aunt Rachel's eighty-fifth birthday party."

"Oh, my goodness! Rachel will be eighty-five? That's amazing. When is her birthday?"

"December 31. She's a New Year's Eve baby. She is literally. As I understand she was born at almost midnight."

"How fun! I don't think I ever knew when her birthday was. Where are you going to have the party? It might be hard to find a location for New Year's Eve."

"That's what I need to talk to you about. I've got a secret."

Jenn spent the next few minutes filling Mel in on the situation with the Oasis being left to the Halston sisters. Even after she stopped talking, Mel continued to sit in front of her in silence with her mouth wide open.

"Say something, Mel."

"Holy jellybeans, I can't believe what you just told me." Mel's eyes continued to bug out. "You three and the Oasis! I get that your families were close. It never occurred to me that they might adopt you!" Mel snorted in laughter.

"I know."

"It's incredible!" Mel lowered her voice. "It's scary."

"It is. Terrifying is really a better word."

"Don't tell me that's where you are planning to have Rachel's party?"

"That's the rest of the secret. We're going to make it into a fundraiser for one of Aunt Rachel's favorite charities."

"Oh, Jenn, that's perfect. I can see Mrs. Bentley smiling. I can't even imagine what the price of a ticket will be. Will I be able to afford it?"

"Oh, you are dating a rich car dealer." Jenn winked. "Seriously, the ticket price will need to be at a certain level. We've not determined that yet. Amber is used to putting these types of events on in California. She says that the price needs to cover all the costs and a little more, but the real fundraising happens when the patrons are having a fabulous time and take out their checkbooks for additional donations as the evening progresses."

"That makes sense."

"We've already secured More Please to be our caterer."

"They are *the* best."

"Amber was also able to secure some other vendors through the destination wedding section on the newspaper website, which I understand comes from your guidebook."

"It does." Mel batted her eyes with pride.

"Even though we are behind, we are ahead because of all the things I've just mentioned. The biggest aspect we are lacking is entertainment."

"Ah, I think that would rival the food aspect."

"Yes, I've told Amber that you have the brain we need to pick for that. Renee and I know no one in that field of work. You know *everyone*."

"I wouldn't say *everyone*."

Jenn gave her a stern look.

"Okay, I do. Thanks for lunch." Mel picked up her phone and got up from the table.

"Where are you going?"

"Jenn, this is November something. I don't even know what day it is. The party is less than two months away. There's no time to waste to find entertainment, which I'm presuming means a band or, at the very least, the most talented piano player in North Carolina and a lovely lady who can belt out the classics. Either way, there's no time to waste. I've got to go search my rolodex."

"Do you still have one of those?"

"Oh, Jenn, don't be silly." Mel walked briskly toward the door, turning before she exited. "Of course, I do! That's where I keep my secret connections."

"I was beginning to get a little worried about you." Jenn smiled to herself, knowing where her daughter had been.

"It takes a while to catch up on a decade." Claire smiled with a faraway look in her eyes. "I guess it's longer than that. I didn't imagine that I would ever see Wade again."

"And now that you have?" Jenn asked the question she hoped would lead her daughter to reveal what was in her heart.

"It makes me a little sad that we didn't keep in better touch." Claire frowned.

"I remember how much you liked him, even beyond the crush of young love." Jenn rubbed her daughter's back as she walked by.

"I was a silly young girl infatuated with Wade, that's for sure. I also enjoyed being his friend. We had some deep conversations about our futures. By the end of that summer, I might have considered Wade to be my best friend."

Jenn watched Claire run her fingers through her long brown hair. The shade was identical to Jenn's, minus the gray that had made an appearance a few years ago. Jenn thought she saw a glimmer in her daughter's green eyes. While it might be too soon for Claire to begin another relationship, Jenn also suspected that her daughter needed a friend, someone neutral and removed from the life she'd left behind.

"I'm sure Gladys is enjoying Wade's visit. Has he begun looking for a place to live?"

"I think she's spoiling him. He mentioned that Gladys has been preparing lots of different food for him, some of his favorites from childhood. I don't think he's started a search for a place to live. He said that his work has been keeping him busy."

Jenn thought for a moment, trying to remember if Wade or Gladys had mentioned what he did for a living. Nothing was quickly coming to mind.

"What does Wade do for a living?"

"His work has something to do with developing teaching curriculum. I believe it's for middle or high school courses." Claire looked intently at her mother. "All these months that you've been here, I wondered why you seem so different, Mom. You've seemed happier in a way that I couldn't put my finger on. It's more than your new life as a publisher or even your romance with Randy. It's like you've sounded renewed. I've been here less than a week and I'm already feeling it. Serendipity casts a spell on your soul. It's in the air. Life is different."

"That's an interesting way to describe it. Your phrasing sounds like something that Mel would use in her marketing. I always knew that my hometown was a special place. I never realized how life changing it could be. I've become a new person here—a truer version of myself than has quite possibly existed anywhere or at any other time in my life."

"You probably know better than anyone that I've been in a hard place for a while. Not totally unhappy, just less happy than I knew I could be. Derek is a wonderful man. I believe, and hope, that he will always be one of my best friends. There was and is love between us. We shouldn't have gotten married though. That type of bond never existed between us. We both refused to believe that. Now we know the truth."

"I've known something was off for a while. I did not want to interfere. Like my own situation with your father, sometimes you need to come to your own realization, in your own time." Jenn pulled Claire into an embrace. "I always thought Derek was a fine young man. I'm glad to hear that you still feel that way. It's good that you both could part amicably. I hope that you can remain friends. A good, strong friend is hard to come by, especially one who intimately understands you."

"We've been working through these feelings for a while. It's been a topic we began discussing on our first anniversary. As I said, there is still love between us. Even though we suspected we might be happier apart, we wanted to be sure. We took our marriage seriously and went into it with the intention of staying together for a lifetime. But life is too short to be anything but happy. You are a great example of how much impact a little happy can make in your life."

Jenn looked deep into her oldest child's eyes. In those pools of green, Jenn saw a little girl and an old woman. It was as if in an instant she saw Claire's entire life. It was interesting. It was happy. It was full of love. *What more could a mother wish for?*

"I hope that you can embrace the possibility that you have been given the chance to hit the 'reset' button. Your new role in the gallery, your new life in Serendipity, maybe these things are laying the groundwork for a world of happy for you."

"Is it crazy that my teenage heart skipped a few beats while I was talking to Wade?" Claire looked down blushing.

"I don't think so. Wade is a charming man. Your feelings for him before were strong. I remember your grandmother telling me about the young love that was blooming on the beach. You came home full of animated stories about him. I was sad when the two of you drifted apart. A long-distance relationship is hard at any point in life, but for teenagers, it's almost impossible." Jenn thought back to the conversation she had with Wade. "When I spoke with him after he first arrived, I don't recall him mentioning whether or not he had a family."

"He doesn't. Wade told me that he's never been married or even engaged." Claire paused for a few moments. "I asked him why."

Good girl. Find out the rest of the story.

"I can't say that I recall Gladys mentioning much about him through the years when I was visiting."

"Wade said that he'd really poured himself into his career. He devoted himself to this international company he works for in the hopes that, if he became a vital member of their team, he could call his own shots later. From the way it sounds, it worked."

"I'm not sure that fully explains him not being in a relationship. Even the biggest workaholics often have a spouse or a family."

"I thought that, too. I'm almost afraid to say his response aloud."

Jenn saw some emotion spring up in her daughter's eyes. She remained silent, waiting for Claire to be ready to continue.

"I also asked him why he decided to move to Serendipity. Of course, it's a beautiful place and living at the beach has its own lure. There are hundreds of coastal towns between here and Boston though. Why did he choose Serendipity?"

"That's a great question. Gladys is here, but if I'm not mistaken, she has another sibling that lives in a coastal community. Even his home in Boston isn't far from the coast."

"Wade said that the happiest time of his life was spent in Serendipity. That no matter where he's gone and what he's done since then, the summer he spent here was his favorite. Wade said that Serendipity was the only place he considered when he found out that he could continue his position from anywhere." Claire began to cry.

"Tell me, Claire."

"Wade said that he hadn't been brave enough to try and find the girl who'd held his heart for so long. But maybe she would find him if he came back to where they'd been so happy together."

"Oh, Claire."

Jenn pulled her sobbing daughter into a comforting hug, rocking her back and forth. She could feel her normally strong daughter letting go in her arms. The pent-up emotion was flowing. Claire's heart was releasing the burdens of the life she'd only recently left behind. After a few minutes, Claire sat up, wiping her tears.

"It's too soon. I'm not even divorced yet. This is crazy. We had a teenage summer romance."

"A year ago, I was saying the same thing. It was too soon. I'd been married for thirty years. I shouldn't rush into another relationship. Had Randy not been a patient and determined man, I might have lost my second chance at the love of my life. I've discovered in the last few months that is who Randy really is. Please understand me. I would not trade the life with your father for anything in the world, because that life gave me the three most important people who will ever grace my existence. Despite all that your father has done, I still have love for him because of that, always."

"I know. We know. Your three amigos understand that."

"I understand now though that I have loved Randy all my life. He's been in my heart, waiting for *our* time. He feels the same. It's not too soon. *It's time.* We are embracing the love that we've both felt and letting it lead us into a new life together." Jenn took hold of Claire's hand. "I'm not saying that's how it will be for you and Wade. It is too soon for you to know that. It's not too soon for you to find out. There's a reason you've both ended up back in Serendipity at the same time. It's more than a happy accident. It was meant to be. Embrace that and see where it takes you. No guilt about the life you left behind. You and Derek made that decision together and are moving on with love in your hearts. That's a sign for both of you. Get the legalities out of the way and move on. When the ink dries on your divorce papers, you will be as divorced as you will ever be."

"Wow, Mom. I never thought I'd be getting divorce advice from you." Claire squeezed Jenn's hand.

"Consider it second chance advice. I've become an expert."

Chapter Fourteen

Rachel

"Your cousins are having a party in my honor for my eighty-fifth trip around the sun."

Rachel sat across from Ross in the dining room. Arriving the day before, they'd spent the previous evening pouring over all the information that Doris and Lyle had gathered about Jordan Rivers. It amazed Rachel how much could be found in such a short period of time. It was enough to give Ross a snapshot of his biological father's existence and confirmed that Jordan Rivers had been deceased for quite a few years.

"My cousins who I am going to meet later today?"

"Yes, I'm afraid they and their families are the only cousins of yours that I know."

"Please tell me their names again and a little about them. That will help me retain whatever I learn directly this afternoon."

"My sister, Paisley, and her husband, Marshall, had three daughters. Renee is the oldest. She is married to Neil. He is a fine man who my father, your grandfather, took under his wing many years ago in the construction business. Father turned Halston Construction over to Neil almost two decades ago. It is Renee and Neil whose son was abducted. Jonah was five years old. It was a horrendous experience. Honestly, so many years had passed, I'd lost all hope that the child would ever be found alive. It was a lesson in not giving up. Joe, as we call him now, was found a couple of months ago, living in the other end of the state. It's a miraculous story. I will let them tell it to you."

"My goodness. I believe I heard that story on the news recently, if I'm thinking of the same situation. Did it make the national news?"

"It made international news. I daresay that the coverage this wonderful story will get has only scratched the surface." Rachel took a drink of coffee. "Joe is their only child. He is living here in Serendipity now and is a police officer. Renee and Neil have a home in Raleigh, but more recently have been spending most of their time here."

"Renee. Neil. Joe. Got it."

"Paisley's second child is Jennifer. We call her Jenn. She lived in Atlanta for most of her adult life until she divorced a little over a year ago. After my beloved Paisley suddenly left us, Jenn inherited the beach house that my father built many years ago. She moved home and bought the local newspaper."

"Yes, the newspaper where Doris works."

"That's correct. Jenn's first job out of college was as a reporter for the *Serendipity Sun*. She left that job for a career in Public Relations in Atlanta and to marry Simon, her first husband. He is the father of her three children, Claire, Foster, and Emily."

"You refer to her first husband, has Jenn remarried?"

"Not yet." Rachel chuckled. "We are all quite fond of her boyfriend though and foresee nuptials in her future."

"He must be a good man for her family to feel that way."

"Randy is one of the best men in this town. Randy Nave is the Chief of Police. We've known him his whole life though. His family were neighbors of Paisley's family. Jenn and Randy grew up together. Her mother and I hoped a romance would bloom while they were younger. Jenn went off to college and met Simon. If you are familiar with the expression, Simon was good on paper."

"Ah, I've heard that term. Someone who has the credentials of a bright future, but not the temperament to match."

"That's what was discovered. I don't suppose any of us would have called him a bad person. Simon never seemed to make our Jenn happy enough. Thankfully, their children were grown before he decided to have his midlife crisis. He left our Jenn for a woman who was close to the same age as his oldest daughter."

"That's a hard one to swallow, I'm sure. I would imagine that would make Jenn cautious about marrying again."

"It probably does. What about you, Ross? Have you ever considered marrying again? I believe you said your wife has been deceased for quite a few years."

"Aretta has been gone for over a decade now. Our children were in their teens when she passed." Ross took a deep breath, frowning. "For the first couple of years, I stayed busy with the kids. It didn't even cross my mind to date anyone. After they were both in college, some of my work colleagues and neighbors started trying to fix me up on blind dates. I went on a few. Most of the women were pleasant. None of them were Aretta though. I married for life. I never imagined that I would become a widower. It usually doesn't work that way."

"That is indeed the rarer of the two possibilities."

"I'm not opposed to the idea of remarrying. Aretta talked about it before she passed. She was in favor of it. I don't believe she could imagine how I would survive by myself. I've done okay though. Conquered the laundry. Developed some decent cooking skills. I don't need a woman to take care of me. I'd like to have a companion. It gets lonely sometimes. I suppose you understand that. I don't believe that you mentioned ever marrying."

"No. Sometime I will tell you about my first love. He and I were engaged. He was killed in military service."

"Oh, I'm sorry to hear that. I appreciate his service to our country."

"Thank you. It was a long time ago. I was still grieving his loss when I met your father. Those two combined situations greatly impacted future decisions I made about relationships. I've often wished that I would have pursued some of the romantic opportunities that came my way. At the same time, I wouldn't have traded the times I had with Richard or Jordan, even now knowing how each ended."

"We are the sum of our experiences, good and bad."

"Indeed. I would have been a far different person if I'd gone down a different path. My career became my focus. I had thousands of students through the years. Many I dearly loved. Quite a few keep in touch with me decades later. I even have a few namesakes as in Rachels and a couple of Fredericks."

"That's nice. Those students must hold you in high regard to name a child after you. You must have made a difference in their lives."

"Each one of those who gave their child my name came from hard homes. I bestowed on each a little extra attention and care. Many in education say that you should not show a preference in one child over another, and I agree with that, mostly. There are some situations though where you know for a certainty that a child is lacking the care he or she needs in the home. You can either step in and provide attention or you can watch that child grow into a statistic. I chose the former to try to prevent the latter." Rachel thought for a moment. "It occurs to me that there is an important aspect of your life which we have yet to discuss. You said you are retired. I do not believe that you shared what your field of work was."

"I guess we've had way too many other things to discuss. I specialized in equipment maintenance. Some people say I can fix anything. I worked for several different factories in the early years of my career, but finally settled with a large hotel chain as the overall corporate Director of Maintenance. By the time I retired, I had a crew of fifty technicians working for me. What I loved most though was getting out in the field doing repair and maintenance myself."

"That sounds like a great deal of responsibility."

"As the years passed, it certainly was. The geographic division I was over included over two hundred and fifty hotel properties. Most of the general preventative maintenance or minor repairs were done by on-property maintenance persons who reported to the hotel's general manager. But if there were large equipment failures, and there always were, it was a member of my crew who would visit the property and make the repair or equipment replacement. As I'm sure you realize, hotels are open twenty-four hours a day, seven days a week, and fifty-two weeks a year. Most of our properties also had some level of restaurant and bar facilities, so that made for even more potential equipment issues."

"How did you get into this type of work? Was your father in a similar vocation?"

"No, my father was a doctor. I'm sure he imagined that I might follow in his footsteps and go to medical school. I didn't have any interest in medicine. But, for as long as I can remember, I've enjoyed taking things apart and figuring out how they go back together. I've always had a mechanical mind."

"Excellent! I applaud you pursuing what you enjoyed instead of what was expected."

"My parents did not pressure me either way. They did insist that I receive an education, so I did earn an engineering degree. The different types of certifications I've completed through the years include a long list in electricity, electronics, building, and the list goes on and on."

"I can't help but wonder if it was some of the genes you inherited from my father that influenced your abilities. He could build or fix anything."

"It's certainly possible. Even from a young age, my mother would often find me in the floor taking some small appliance apart. My father was not handy at all in that way. My mother quickly put me under the tutelage of our next-door neighbor who was an appliance repairman by profession. I became Mr. Crosby's helper." Ross shook his head, smiling. "I learned as much from that man as I did in four years of college. He was amazing."

"Hands-on education is usually a more powerful learning tool than anything you can learn from a textbook. That's coming from someone who holds a PhD in education."

"It does sound like I would have gotten along well with your father. I'm thankful for whomever I received my inclination from toward the mechanical side of life." Ross looked at his watch. "If it's okay with you, I think I will go back to my hotel and rest a little while before I meet my cousins this evening. All that we learned about Jordan yesterday kept dancing in my head last night. I didn't get the best sleep. Maybe a nap and a shower would make me more alert and energetic for this meeting."

"That will be fine." Rachel chuckled. "Keep in mind that you don't have to 'play' with your cousins this evening, so you don't need to be too energetic. You will need to be mentally sharp though. These three girls are quick-witted and will probably attack you with many questions."

"Thanks for the warning. I need that nap then."

"I wish you would have stayed here. I have so much room."

"I promise to take you up on that the next time. I am amazed at how comfortable I am starting to feel." Ross reached over and took Rachel's hand. "I hoped that would be the case eventually, but I didn't expect it to come so quickly." Releasing her hand, he rose and began walking to the door.

"Have a good nap. Doris will be arriving mid-afternoon to help me with dinner preparations. I believe the girls will be here by six."

A few moments later, Rachel heard the click of the front door close. A tear rolled down her cheek. Looking at the hand that Ross had just held, she remembered that same hand being held by his father. It seemed so long ago. *It seems like yesterday.*

"Rachel, I really think that five types of salad dressing are sufficient. You are not opening a restaurant. I don't believe that anyone in attendance this evening is that finicky."

Rachel watched her friend, Doris, scurry from one end of the kitchen to another. She wished her legs were still that limber. Mobility was slower for Rachel than she imagined it would be, even at eighty-five.

"I know. I just want things to be perfect. It's such a glorious time for my son, I still haven't gotten used to saying that, to meet my nieces. I have loved them as much as if they'd been my own, you know."

"I do know and so do they. Jenn has been anxious all week about meeting Ross. She's asked me a dozen questions about him. I keep telling her that my knowledge is limited." Doris suddenly stopped in the middle of the kitchen. "Are you sure that it's okay for me to be here this evening? I feel like I'm intruding on a special family moment."

"Good grief, Doris. As a family member yourself, I don't see how you being here can be an intrusion."

Rachel's frown turned into a stifled giggle when her eyes caught a glimpse of Doris' shoes. The bright pink strapless heels were adorned with a fluffy powderpuff-like embellishment over the toes. They looked like boudoir slippers from a decade long ago, which meant they were perfect with her vintage-loving friend's ensemble.

"Let's go over the menu one more time. I keep thinking I've forgotten something." Rachel looked at her list on the counter. "The pork medallions are simmering in the oven. The mashed potatoes are staying warm in the crockpot. Green beans are cooking on the stove, along with asparagus."

"There's also cranberry chutney, gravy for the potatoes, and yeast rolls ready to bake."

"I don't believe you told me what delectable flavor of cake you've so kindly made for the occasion."

"It's an Italian cream cake with strawberries."

"You are spoiling us."

"It is a celebration. I think there's time enough for you to lay down for a few minutes. Why don't you do that while I set the table?"

"A little rest would be nice. Are you sure?"

"I'm so sure that I might just stretch out on the couch and do the same thing myself. Go on." Doris began to shoo Rachel out of the room. "Everything is basically ready, except for the rolls."

Despite Rachel's guilt, she welcomed the opportunity to stretch out on her bed for a little while. She wanted to enjoy every minute of the time with her family. A little rest would go a long way toward making that possible.

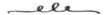

"We don't want to dwell on what might have been, Ross, but you may have dodged a bullet not having to grow up with us." Renee's blunt statement caught Rachel off-guard.

"Why do you say that?" Ross passed the basket of rolls back to Doris who was seated next to him.

"The Halston sisters might have terrorized a male cousin if we'd had access to one. Our father had two nephews, but they were both over fifteen years older than me. The rest of our cousins were girls."

"Ah, well, maybe since I am a little older than you, Renee, I would have been the one doing the terrorizing."

Rachel was pleased with how easily the conversation had progressed between Ross and his three cousins. As they reached the end of the meal, it seemed more like it had been a decade since the four had conversed rather than the lifetime which had actually passed.

"You have that Halston spunk, Ross." Jenn smiled broadly. "You shall fit into this family just fine. We're happy to have you."

"I'm happy to hear that. When I began this quest, I never expected to gain more than a little knowledge about my heritage. I didn't expect to be welcomed into a family. I suppose that I didn't dare hope for that much."

"As we briefly told you, we have a little recent experience with welcoming those who have been long gone from our sight." Renee wiped a quick tear. "It still makes this mother emotional."

"Indeed. It is a glorious story. I was filled with joy when I heard it, as a stranger, on the news. I'm thrilled to know that I may call this young man my cousin. My children and I discussed the situation when it broke in the news. They remembered how extra protective it made their mother when the incident occurred two decades ago. They also reminded me that our church held a meal fundraiser and sent the proceeds to the efforts to find your son."

"Oh, my goodness." Renee placed her hand over her heart. "We were fortunate that funds came in from all over the country for those efforts. I never imagined that I would meet a stranger who made a donation." Renee reached across the table for Ross' hand. "Thank you."

"Renee, the ordeal that you and your husband endured touched a chord with parents everywhere. The blessing of Jonah being found will be felt in the hearts of many."

"Ross, we are happy that you are planning to come to the party for Aunt Rachel. It will be a very festive night. You're going to need to rent a tuxedo, if you don't own one." Jenn winked.

"That festive! It's been many years since I've needed to dress so formally. That does indeed sound like a fancy affair."

"Yes, it does. That's a little fancier than I imagined." A stern look crossed Rachel's face. There was something she hadn't been told. "Jenn, would you care to explain where it is going to be held?"

"We probably should have already revealed the location to you, Aunt Rachel. We were hoping to have some more concrete official news."

Rachel watched a look pass between the three sisters. *They're up to something.*

"You heard Pattie, the paperwork is almost complete. It probably would already be official, if it wasn't for the international aspects."

Amber's comments only added confusion in Rachel's mind.

"Aunt Rachel looks like she's about to blow a fuse." Renee nudged Rachel from her seat beside her. "Doris, stop gathering the dishes and sit down. We can have dessert after we tell you this story. No one needs to have cake in their mouth when they hear this news. It's unbelievable."

About fifteen minutes later, Renee and Jenn finished their animated story of how it was now coming to pass that the Halston sisters were inheriting the Oasis. Rachel sat in stunned silence, trying to absorb the details. She couldn't help but chuckle under her breath at the expression on Ross' face. Even though he'd never seen the mansion, he seemed to somewhat understand the magnitude of the estate and its incredible value.

"Say something, Aunt Rachel." Jenn's wide-eyed comment diverted Rachel's attention away from Ross.

"Ross, you will definitely need a tuxedo."

The entire table howled at her response, causing Rachel to join them in laughter.

"Don't take this the wrong way, I'm happy that the Bentleys both lived long lives. I've got to be honest though, I'm a little disappointed that Paisley and I didn't have the opportunity to inherit that beautiful estate, *but* we might not have ranked as high in Walter's eyes as the three of you did. You three most certainly had granddaughter status."

"My goodness, what will you three do with that huge house?" Doris appeared to be still reacting to the news. "Jenn, you already have a newspaper to run. We can't be losing you to this shiny new thing."

"No worries about that, Doris. My life savings and I are fully committed to making the *Serendipity Sun* successful for many years to come. We've not firmly decided on anything yet, but we have been toying with the idea of turning it into a high-end resort. Especially since one of us has some experience at that." Jenn looked at Amber.

"Oh, I'd forgotten. Ross, Amber ran a swanky resort in California. It catered to the rich and famous set. It's where she met her husband."

"Is your husband rich and famous? More surprises in this family? That would be shocking." Ross rolled his eyes.

"Amber's husband used to play baseball." Rachel replied, shaking her head.

"It was basketball, Aunt Rachel, and he's currently my ex-husband." Amber turned to Ross. "My addiction issues, that I briefly mentioned earlier, led to our divorce. He's never given up on me and is a wonderful father to our son. We are planning to remarry."

"Oh, my kids and I are big basketball fans. You are speaking of the NBA, I presume."

"Yes. Have you ever heard of Dawson Hyder?"

"Of course I have." A shocked look crossed Ross' face. "I've not been hiding under a rock for the last twenty years. He's one of the greats. His career was cut short too soon by an automobile accident that messed up his knees. I guess you're about to tell me that he's my cousin-in-law."

"Yes." Amber smiled from ear-to-ear.

"I've told my children that they have a new family to meet in the future. I believe they are looking forward to that. They will be thrilled to learn that my family tree includes so many interesting branches."

"May I be so forward as to ask if they can come to this special party at the beautiful house?"

"Absolutely! We will make sure there are tickets reserved for you and whomever you'd like to bring." Renee clapped her hands. "You must come in before then though, so that the rest of the family can meet you as well. I may be speaking out of turn, Aunt Rachel."

"It would not be the first time, my dear." Rachel winked at Renee. "Speak freely, we are *all* family in this room."

"This Christmas is going to be one of the happiest and saddest for our family, Ross. It will be happy because of the many people who have been reunited over the last year as well as the fact that some of us have not lived within close geographical proximity for many years. It will also be sad, because this will be our first Christmas without our beloved mother, your aunt. We would be honored if you and your family would consider being with us during the holidays to celebrate and remember so many blessings, which now include you."

Rachel's heart swelled at the beauty of Renee's words. *The truth was overwhelming.*

CHAPTER FIFTEEN

Jenn

"I WAS RATHER SURPRISED when Aunt Renee said that she and Uncle Neil were going to stay in Raleigh after they dropped off Aunt Amber at the airport." Claire sat at the kitchen counter, stirring her coffee.

"Renee mentioned to me about a week ago that since we had plans for a big Christmas here, they wanted to have a quiet Thanksgiving with Joe at the house in Raleigh. I believe they are thinking about selling that house and moving closer to Serendipity."

"Oh, it's hard to imagine them permanently leaving Raleigh."

"All those years that Joe was missing, I think they felt like they had to stay where he'd last lived. It was part of not giving up on his return. Now, they are realizing that Joe has almost no memories of that house. He doesn't feel a connection to it. Renee says that it became a sad place for her and Neil as time went by. I think they're ready for a fresh start. Neil seems to like Tyrell County where he's been working on that large construction project. He's indicated the phases of that project will take him through at least the next five years. That timeline will put them close to retirement."

"What will that mean for Halston Construction? Do you think he will completely retire? Uncle Neil has always been such a worker."

"I could see him going into semi-retirement, especially if he can convince Dawson to step into a role in the company."

"Oh, I had forgotten that Uncle Dawson is in the construction business, too. My strongest memories of him are when Dad used to take us to see him whenever he was playing in Atlanta."

"Those were good times. From what I understand, Dawson has a prosperous construction company in California, but he also has a couple of partners who are willing to take over running the business if Dawson decides to relocate to this coast."

"That makes sense if Aunt Amber is going to run the Oasis. She seems so focused on the idea now. Planning Aunt Rachel's birthday party has really reinvigorated her desire to work in that field."

"I agree. It also gives me hope that with such a focus and having almost all her family nearby, it will strengthen her on a path to a firm recovery."

"I hope so. She seems happy. I am sure that will only improve when Willis enrolls in school here after the Christmas break." Claire continued to drink her coffee, while scrolling on her phone. "What are we going to do for Thanksgiving? It's only a few days away. I lost track of time when I made that quick trip to New York last week."

"Foster and Michelle are going to Atlanta to spend a few days with Michelle's family. Am I right that Michelle's brother and his wife are expecting their first child?"

"Yes. That's Taylor and Josie. Josie's had a difficult pregnancy, and the doctor isn't letting her travel until the baby arrives in January. Michelle is helping her mother host a baby shower on the Saturday after Thanksgiving."

"Yes, I sent a present with them. Michelle seems excited." Jenn made a couple of notes on the grocery list she started the day before. "I think Joe is going to split his time between being in Raleigh with his parents and having a holiday meal with Megan's family. I think he is off some of this weekend because most of Randy's team will be working downtown during the Christmas Parade and other festivities."

"That's when the newspaper's Open House is being held, right? You've got me down to help Doris with the refreshments?"

"Yes, I appreciate your willingness to help."

"I guess we should consider the *Serendipity Sun* to be part of the family business. With the Oasis added to that, it's really going to be a diversified portfolio."

"Don't forget your brother's condo business, and we are still semi-partners in Halston Construction." Jenn put her hand on her forehead. "That makes my head hurt. We are a family going in a lot of directions."

"It's a good thing there are plenty of us."

"Back to your question, I was planning on having a quiet dinner here on Thanksgiving. I've invited Randy, Aunt Rachel, and Doris, and was thinking about asking Gladys and Wade, if you are okay with that." Jenn casually watched her daughter's reaction. Jenn knew the two had met a couple of times, but Claire hadn't discussed him any further.

"I was about to ask you that very thing. When we last talked, Wade mentioned that he would be here for Thanksgiving, but that he and Gladys were making plans to fly to Boston to have Christmas with his parents and other family."

"I think I will walk over to see Gladys in a few minutes then and extend the invitation. It will be nice to have a quiet Thanksgiving. This house will be a zoo during Christmas and New Year's."

"Sounds good. I'm going to head back to my condo. Jocelyn and I have a conference call with a gallery in Australia."

"My international daughter, always doing business with someone on another continent."

"That's my life. I'm thankful that the internet allows me to not constantly have to be in an airport." Claire kissed Jenn on the cheek before heading out the door.

Jenn spent the next quiet hour straightening up the kitchen and doing a load of laundry. It felt strange to be all alone in her house. A text from Randy let her know that he was on his way to represent his police department at the funeral of a fellow Police Chief in South Carolina.

"Jasper, let's take a walk and see if our friend Gladys is home."

Rising from his big pillow, Jasper's tail was quickly wagging at the prospect of going outside. Late November was an unpredictable time weatherwise on the coast. One day might be warm and sunny, the next might bring blustery winds that would make the ocean breeze feel frigid. The clear sky gave Jenn hope that she and Jasper might have an enjoyable walk on the beach and perhaps Gladys would join them.

Jasper skipped down the steps in front of her and was heading in the direction of Gladys' house before Jenn could catch up.

"Hello!" Gladys' greeting came from above.

Jenn looked up to see her neighbor waving her bright yellow sunhat.

"Want to go for a walk?" Jenn shaded her eyes, looking up at Gladys.

"That's where I was heading. I'll be right down."

Jenn watched Jasper sniffing the tires of Gladys' vehicle while Jenn waited for her neighbor to walk down the steps from the deck. She noticed that Wade's sporty car was not in its usual spot.

"The celestial deity aligned our cosmic communication so that we could simultaneously desire to breathe in the ocean air."

"Yes." Jenn could not think of any other way to respond.

Gladys was in full Gladys-form from her bright yellow sunhat and dark movie star sunglasses to the orange and white polka dot yoga outfit and neon green tennis shoes. Her 'statement from the Universe' completed the ensemble.

"I'm glad to see that Jasper will be joining us. I've been thinking about asking a member of his species to move in with me. It would be an adoption, of course. I will not support the puppy mill industry and the exploitation of our canine brothers and sisters."

"There are several reputable animal rescue groups in the area. There's a column in the newspaper which highlights current animals that are available."

Gladys and Jenn reached the beach with Jasper frolicking in front of them. Gladys immediately began power walking like she was doing laps in a city park.

"Yes, I noticed that in the last edition of the *Serendipity Sun*."

"Happy to hear that you didn't cancel your subscription when it was bought by a Halston." Jenn hoped that Gladys was in the mood to banter.

"You think you are being funny. It would not have been unheard of for a long-term friend and pseudo-family member to receive a complimentary subscription as a kind neighborly gesture."

"Oh, Gladys, that never even occurred to me. You are right. There are several people who I should probably send subscriptions."

"Jennifer Halston! Don't you dare! I was trying to go toe-to-toe in a snark match with you. I am thrilled to financially support your entrepreneur woman-powered enterprise!" Gladys raised her fists in the air to punctuate her point. "I probably should order several subscriptions!"

"Gladys Fox! Don't you dare! I was volleying that snark right back at you, sister! Free subscriptions are not something I can afford this early in my newspaper game, but I appreciate each and every *one* of the subscribers."

"I am *so* proud of you. All your ancestors are sending daily rays of sunshine with their smiles."

"Oh, Gladys, that's such a wonderful thing to say. Thank you. It's a great segway to the reason I was heading over to your house this morning. I have an invitation for you."

"An invitation for me!" Gladys stopped walking, taking hold of Jenn's arms. "You are going to marry that yummy delicious Chief Randy, aren't you? You are going to get married at sunrise as seagulls swoop for their breakfast. Will there be bagpipes? I love men in kilts."

Jenn closed her eyes, shaking her head, trying to process what Gladys said.

"Slow down, Gladys. I'm not getting married. I wanted to invite you to have Thanksgiving with us."

"Oh, but I want you to take your vows with Randy as you parasail into the sunset like one of those floats in the Macy parade."

Gladys' descriptions of possible wedding scenarios were starting to jumble in Jenn's head. She knew that they would most likely show up in Jenn's dreams one night.

"That sounds interesting, Gladys. Why don't we have Thanksgiving first and then see what happens?"

"You're right. It's already on the calendar for this week. We can't forget the Pilgrims. I will make my stuffed squash and cranberry bread. Can my 'Plus One' be Wade? I must warn you, he's quite the eater."

Without any warning, Gladys turned around and began briskly walking in the direction toward their houses. Jenn almost fell in the sand, trying to catch up with her.

"I would be delighted for Wade to come. I think Claire would enjoy him being there very much."

Jenn continued walking ahead, not realizing that Gladys had stopped again. Turning back, she saw that Gladys was facing the ocean.

"I think the two of them fell in love right here on this beach when they were on the verge of adulthood. Their hearts became bound together like the way coral sticks to a reef. Fate tried to keep them apart. It almost succeeded."

"Young love does grab hold of you sometimes." Jenn watched the waves crashing on the horizon. It was powerful to watch and relaxing to feel.

"It grabbed hold of a girl and a boy on this beach a dozen years ago. It did the same to the girl's mother and another handsome fellow in a neighborhood a few miles from here about forty years or so ago. Life has a way of being too fast and too slow all at once. It's the reason why people miss some life-changing moments sometimes. They are looking ahead when they should be paying attention to what just happened."

"That's so true, Gladys."

"Of course it is, Jenn." Gladys began to power walk again. "Truth pours out of me like sweat. See you later. *The Price is Right* reruns are about to come on. That Bob Barker is such a hunk."

Jenn laughed aloud, watching her colorful senior friend walk like a teenager back to her house. Even Jasper couldn't keep up with her, so he was waiting at the bottom of the stairs until the bright yellow sunhat was out of sight.

"Mel says she's booked a band for Aunt Rachel's party, but she won't tell me who it is."

Amber's first words on their FaceTime call caught Jenn off-guard.

"Why won't she tell you?" Jenn furrowed her brow.

"She says that it's a surprise and for us not to worry; she would never let Aunt Rachel down."

"I believe that. I'd really like for it not to be a night of surprises, at least not for us."

"I know. Organizers need to know every minute part of an event. The devil is in the details. We need to know everything so that zero problems arise."

Jenn watched Amber tap her pen on the side of her head. It was a mannerism Amber developed in childhood that signaled she was trying to figure something out. It was the most 'Amber thing' Jenn had seen her little sister do since she'd gotten out of rehab. She could almost hear their mother saying, 'Don't tap your head, Amber.' The simple little nuance filled Jenn's heart with joy.

"I'm not going to worry about it." Amber put the pen down. "I trust Mel. She's the big sister I always wanted." Amber giggled.

"I was feeling a lot of love for you until you said that." Jenn stuck her tongue out.

"Who do you suppose it is? Maybe you could ask Sinclair."

"You are not going to give this up, are you? Mel knows so many entertainers in the area; I bet she has a file full of potential bands. She won't let us down. Did she indicate how much this mystery band is going to cost us?"

"That was the other part of her message that was shocking. She said that the entertainment was being donated. When the band found out in whose honor the party was being held, they said it would be their pleasure to give a complimentary show."

"That price fits our budget!" Jenn did an air high-five toward the computer screen. "What else do you need help confirming?"

"Nothing. The only thing left on my list is the receipt of the RSVPs. Those are going straight to Doris. Megan helped me set up a bank account for the event before I came back to California. Doris is making those deposits as she receives them. Your bestie, Mel, also got us a big donation from her boyfriend."

"Oh, I figured that Sinclair would step up. He used to mow every lawn in Rachel's neighborhood when we were growing up."

"He wrote a big check. He's a platinum sponsor."

"This is really coming together."

"It is. I think it's going to be a great step in launching the Oasis as a special event location, if we decide to use it that way."

"We will have a wonderful event for our beloved Aunt Rachel, and it will be an ideal way for us to 'test the waters,' so to speak, without completely committing to do events like this all the time. I think we should keep our options open."

"Yes, I'd like to study the market and learn the latest trends for the use of mega mansions these days."

"Renee and I are relieved that you want to come home and work with us on this project."

"You two have way more confidence in my ability than I do. So much has changed in this industry, I feel like I'm starting over."

"Starting over can be a good thing, a positive step."

"I know. Starting over with your sisters beside you is the best step I can imagine."

"I feel like I'm going to have to get some new uniforms."

Randy handed Jenn the last plate to load in the dishwasher.

"Have your uniforms worn out?" Jenn thought it was a strange topic for Randy to suddenly bring up.

"No, mine are only a few months old."

"Why will you need new ones then?" Maybe she was having 'Thanksgiving brain' from cooking since early that morning. Jenn wasn't following Randy's thought process.

"After that delicious dinner, mine aren't going to fit anymore. I feel like I ate enough for three people."

"You certainly consumed portions worthy of this festive day." Jenn laughed. "But Wade ate like this was his last meal."

"I'm happy to hear *you* say that. Since this was my first time meeting Wade, I didn't want to be the one who commented on his healthy appetite. The boy can eat."

"Gladys mentioned to me that he was a hearty eater. Perhaps he loves Thanksgiving food, too."

"There wasn't anything on that table that wasn't worth loving. There wasn't anyone around that table who wasn't worth loving either." Randy winked. "Wade must work out to keep that physique of his. He couldn't keep his eyes off Claire. I take it they have a history?"

"Oh, I forgot that you don't know. Yes, there's a history, a teenage one." Jenn poured two glasses of wine. "Let's put on a jacket and sit on the deck. I think the moon is almost full."

"Sounds almost as lovely as you. I'll get our jackets."

A few minutes later, Jenn and Randy were sitting in side-by-side loungers with a blanket over their legs, sipping wine and gazing at the moon in the clear night sky.

"For a couple of summers when they were teens, Claire and Foster spent their vacations here with my parents. During one of those times, Wade came and stayed with Gladys. As you heard this evening in the conversation, Wade's family lives in Boston. Foster and Wade surfed. Claire and Wade fell in love. My mother gave me an almost daily account of the romance progressing. It sounded quite sweet, but this mother was worried, nonetheless. The summer ended and everyone went home. Claire and Wade exchanged emails and phone calls for a while, but after a year or so, Wade was off to college. I don't believe they connected again until a few weeks ago."

"Both of them ended up back in Serendipity at the same time after all those years?"

"Yes, just like in a movie."

"Claire's divorce is almost final, and Wade's never been married."

"It seems like fate, doesn't it?"

"It seems like we might have to change the name of our town to Second Chances." Randy put his arm around Jenn, pulling her close.

"I want her to be head over heels in love with someone who is worthy of her heart." Jenn kissed Randy on the cheek. "Just like her mother is."

"That's music to my ears. I hope one day soon you'll be ready to discuss our relationship getting more serious."

A twinge of anxiety passed over Jenn. Her life was constantly moving. There were so many big projects. She felt like she was missing something important. The feeling shocked her.

"You're being mighty quiet. I wish I could see your expression better in the moonlight."

"I'm sorry, I guess I'm tired. It's been a long day." Jenn bit her bottom lip, trying to think of something else to say. *I don't like this feeling. What's wrong with me?*

"Okay. I can certainly believe that. The meal was outstanding. You worked way too hard."

"I've got to get back in 'holiday cooking shape.' It's been a couple of years since I've cooked a big holiday meal. My last few years in Atlanta, the kids were going in so many different directions that I didn't do any big meals. This Christmas will be even more elaborate because I believe that my *entire* family will be here."

"You've had several family dinners here already that stretched the fire hazard capacity of this house."

"Okay, Mr. Chief, don't play the fire hazard card if you plan to eat this Christmas. The difference in those dinners and Christmas is that there are more types of food that will be on the menu. The desserts alone will probably fill a table. Don't you remember the table of sweets my mother used to have during the holidays?"

"I remember that incredible spread of deliciousness."

"I'll be preparing recipes from Paisley's cookbook." Jenn took a deep breath. Sadness filled her heart for a moment. "It's going to be a busy month prepping for Christmas. Then Aunt Rachel's party will be a few days later."

"I think I heard Rachel say something about her party today. It sounds like you and your sisters are embracing this idea of owning the Oasis."

"I guess we better. It appears to be only a matter of time before all the legalities are complete. I am enjoying getting to know Pattie Maxwell in the process."

"That doesn't surprise me. Pattie seems like a good person. Maybe you two can become friends."

"I think the Halston sisters are on the road to adopting her. When she gave us a tour of the Oasis the other day, she felt like one of us."

"You can't have too many friends, especially lawyer ones when you have multiple businesses." Randy rose from the lounger, putting both his and Jenn's glasses on the side table, before extending his hand to help her up.

"I know. Claire mentioned the other day about how many different businesses our extended family is involved in. There must be something in the air." Jenn began to turn to walk into the house. "It's mind-boggling. I don't know how I got here."

Randy took hold of her arm, pulling her back to face him. Looking up at him in the moonlight, Jenn could see his eyes twinkling. A slight smile formed on his lips.

"I know how you got here. Every night for as long as I can remember, I've said a prayer that you would come back to me. I think the man upstairs got tired of hearing me. My wish came true."

Softly and slowly, Randy kissed Jenn. Her heart skipped a beat. A calm washed over her.

I know what's in the air. It's love.

About the Author

Attributing her limitless imagination to growing up as an only child, Liza Lanter enjoys creating heartwarming fiction with characters who instantly seem like friends and have bonds that feel like family. Every aspect of her life has involved writing of a non-fiction variety. Her heart is most at home spinning yarns of a fictional nature.

To sign up for Liza's newsletter and learn more about
her writing adventures,
visit www.LizaLanter.com.

Visit the Liza Lanter author page on Amazon
at www.amazon.com/author/lizalanter

Visit the Liza Lanter Facebook page
at http://www.facebook.com/lizalanter

Did you enjoy this book? You can make a big difference by leaving a short review. Honest reviews help convince prospective readers to take a chance on an author they do not know. Thank you.

Made in the USA
Coppell, TX
14 July 2024

34578399R00142